All eyes were on Scully and Red. Before Red could raise his arm to protect his face, Scully's fist landed with the force of a brick. Red had all he could do to stay on his feet but he was too weak and crashed into a table as drinks spilled everywhere!

Blood trickled from Red's eye. He got up slowly as if defeated, but quickly picked up a wooden chair and crashed it into Scully's groin as fast as a bullet. He doubled with pain shooting through his balls as Clara screamed his name.

Scully and Red kept tearing into each other with all the fury and anger within them as other fights broke out all over the room. Scully grabbed a nearby pool stick and drove it into the pit of Red's stomach. "You bastard," Red groaned through clenched teeth.

The sounds of doors being slammed open was heard seconds before two white cops rushed into the club with guns ready to kill a nigger. Hatred for blacks was written all over their faces and silence swept through the bloodied room. It just wasn't Saturday night unless some poor black didn't have his head bashed in by a cop!

—*BLACK STARLET*

Dedicated to my husband Samuel Vance,
to my parents Robert and Alleyne
Booker, and to Michael Kellar.

Bobbye B. Vance

Black Starlet

by Bobbye B. Vance

An Original Holloway House Edition

HOLLOWAY HOUSE PUBLISHING COMPANY

LOS ANGELES, CALIFORNIA

... I

Saturday night for black folks in Gary, Indiana isn't much different from Saturday night for black folks in any other city or town. Whether it's Gary's mid-town area or Atlanta's southwest area. The folks do like to get down. Workin' for the man builds up unwanted pressures and strains.

It's the night for letting the week's frustrations rise through the pores and excape with the funky sweat released in hot, smoky clubs. Bumpin' and grindin', singin' and drinkin', bullshittin' and lovin' on Saturday night takes away all the problems of the week. The only good thing that matters is feeling good about yourself and making yourself feel good.

With the exception of four years at the university, Clara Brown had spent most of her twenty-three years in Gary. She had seen blacks migrate from the South with hopes of finding better jobs. In Gary, steel was the main industry. Many men were able to find decent paying jobs, while women worked as domestics. The hours in the steel mills may not have been as long as the hours in the cotton fields, but the sweat was the same. And it didn't take long to find out that the cracker in the North wasn't much different from the cracker in the South.

Clara could remember her father talking about his young days in South Georgia. The nearest town was ten miles away. That let everyone know that he lived in the country.

"Why, in the South, they don't care how close ya get. It's how big ya get," the light-skinned slim man would say through his small lips which were shaped more like white folks' than blacks'. "And in the North, them bastards don't care how big you get. It's how close you get that worries the hell out of them!"

Clara always remembered his words and put herself above most blacks. She wanted more than Gary had to offer, but returned home after her last year in college to help with the campaign of the black candidate for mayor. She organized the youth by using her talents in drama and music. It didn't take long before over thirty-five teenagers were putting on performances in all parts of the city to raise money and get people out to vote.

A year had passed and the olive brown beauty had become restless. Working in a paper factory by day and with the theatre group by night just wasn't enough to satisfy her and the sweltering summer heat didn't help matters.

As she fumbled for her key to unlock the door of her one bedroom apartment off Broadway, she hated the thought of what this Saturday night might bring.

"One hundred dollars a month for this dump," she thought to herself. Black folks were moving into the Tolliston area but she just didn't want to get too comfortable in Gary. Besides, her man, Scully, was about to find a place and she had just about decided to move in with him. They had met when she moved in and it wasn't long before their casual dates led to the bed.

Scully was a steel worker, but hustling drugs was his main gig. He dug Clara so much that he never got her involved. So whatever deals he had to make were made without her knowing about them. Sometimes, she'd ask him to give it up, but he would say that everyone had to have something on the side. So that ended that.

Clara hadn't dated any white men. But she knew that blacks didn't waste much time with dinner by candlelight. They were into getting high and getting it on! Scully was aggressive! But his approach was a little slower than most. That was because he knew he wasn't dealing with someone out for kicks.

Clara couldn't stand his arrogance and conceit. But Scully was a lover. His six feet, one hundred ninty-five pound mahogany frame met her needs and soothed her desires. Just the thought of the weight of his muscular body pressing against her sent a warm tingle through her body. Tonight, staying home would have pleased her but she knew that Scully wouldn't have that. She didn't stop to pull back the mint green drapes that shut out the city's noise. Instead, she hurried through her small living room down the narrow hall and into the white tiled bathroom. The sweat of day had seeped into her clothings and the hot shower would be a welcome relief.

She pulled her red plaid cotton dress over her head causing her hair to fall wildly over her eyes. Her black bra and bikini panties soon fell to the floor and lay softly at her ankles. She smiled as she looked at herself in the mirror.

"Wild child, your mama should see you now!" Her mother used to tease her about her small breasts.

"Clara, you ain't never gonna have no tits!"

Her crudeness often embarrassed Clara but the skinny teenager was determined to prove to her mother that she would not be flat-chested all her life. Every night Clara would do exercises to build up her breasts. She would place her hands on the sides of the door jamb and push together as hard as she could for a few seconds. She would lower them to eye level and repeat the same exercise. Then she would lower them closer to her waist and repeat the exercise again.

In time her determination paid off. Anytime she made up her mind to do something, she usually did it.

Her large dark brown eyes sparkled through the strands of long hair. Her smooth skin curved in neatly at her waist, widening into the well-rounded hips and buttocks that Scully loved to feel.

"Clara Brown," she chuckled to herself, "you're one helluva woman. Hollywood is waiting for you!"

The hot water beating against her breasts and stomach was soothing. The small bathroom, only big enough to turn around in, quickly became filled with steam. Puffy soap suds covered her body. She turned away from the shower nozzle to rinse her back. Wetting her hair in the shower had always left her with a tingling sensation but she could not afford to get it wet tonight. Instead, she managed to keep it out of the direction of the hot spray. Beads of water covered her body as she quickly turned off the shower. The plastic curtain held back the steam but now, as she moved it to one side, she was blanketed in a heavy fog of steam. She stepped onto a yellow terrycloth bath mat and felt her way to the door. Clara always locked the bathroom door. She remembered the bathroom scene in the movie, *Psycho* and feared an intruder.

The steam was soon replaced by cool air as Clara patted her wet body with a soft yellow towel. She quickly splashed on her favorite perfume. A loud knock was heard at the front door. It couldn't be Scully because he had a key.

"Who is it?" she yelled loudly.

"Me," replied the cocky voice.

"Why in the hell don't you use your key?" she asked as she loosely wrapped the towel around her wet body. Scully mumbled something, but she couldn't hear him.

"O.K., nigger," she said impatiently, "I'm coming as fast as I can. How many times have I told you that you can't tear down a steel door!"

Scully stood in the doorway with one arm raised, ready to knock again. But the sight of Clara, drenched with Aphrodesia, soothed his impatience.

Clara tried to act like a cold black at times, but underneath she was quite warm. And seeing her man standing tall and looking fine in his Pierre Cardin suit calmed her arrogance.

"Hi, honey," she said warmly.

She could barely get the words out of her mouth when Scully's lips were pressing against her small lips. She could feel every muscle of his body pressing against hers and she returned his kisses with all the love in her.

The door closed and the towel fell at the same time. Scully's hands were so warm that Clara wanted them to caress her entire body. Her thin long fingers slowly moved across his buttocks causing him to grind his body into hers. Clara was almost embarrassed at the fast rate of her heartbeat. She wanted Scully as much as he wanted her. Right here on the olive green carpet was as good a place as any.

"Scully," she whined as he slowly guided her to the softness below. Passion was rising as Scully hurriedly stripped. Within moments he lay on top of her, stroking her breasts and moving his strong hand between her hot thighs.

2...

Business was especially good this Saturday night
at the Social Club near Taft and Eleventh Avenue.
The odor of hot sweaty bodies mixed with cigarette smoke as the pool balls rolled across a pool
table at the opposite end of the room.

The Social Club was a favorite spot for Gary's
black steel workers. They were ready to spend a
week's pay on liquor, women, and whatever else
passed by and was ripe for the hustlers and prosti-
tutes that hung out at the club. But it didn't
matter because it was Saturday night. The social
Club was only for those who wanted to gig. If they
couldn't hold their liquor or aim straight, they had
to be ready to deal with whatever followed.

By Bobbye B. Vance

All shades of black swayed and moaned to the music blasting from the large speakers as the trio played the blues.

The club seemed quite small as more people crowded in to find the few remaining tables. By eleven o'clock, standing room was just as scarce. The blues came through the speakers loud and clear as Shorty Ray belted out a Bobby Blue Bland number. "The eagle flies on Friday, and Saturday, I go out to play," sang Shorty as the crowd screamed with "right on!" Nobody in Gary could sing the blues like Shorty! The beady-eyed chubby black man was drenched in sweat as he sang the way they wanted to hear it—slow and easy.

Even though many seemed to be into their own thing, they knew damn well what Short was singing! Black folks have developed the art of talking and listening to music in a noisy club at the same time and doing both quite well.

An "Amen!" or "Preach, Brother, Preach," could be heard often among the chatter and laughter. Everybody had lived the blues and Shorty sang to help ease their burden and forget the white man and his six day a week pressures. The music and liquor were a needed release—so mellow, so nice, a feeling white folks could never know because it comes from way down deep in the bowels, inherited by generations of an oppressed race.

13

The waitresses squeezed between customers, quite often rubbing their buttocks against shoulders or backs. The calls for drinks kept them moving and the manager stood near a pinball machine located in the corner to get a better view of his workers. Big J.A. worked the hell out of his waitresses. Many had quit, but most stayed with him because jobs were scarce and the tips were good.

As Big J.A. watched them take their orders to the long bar that reached twenty feet on one side of the room, he remembered the time when he wanted to remodel the club and hire all young, attractive waitresses. He soon changed his mind when business picked up. A faithful customer hipped him to the fact that nobody could enjoy themselves if it wasn't hot and stinky, crowded and smoky. The waitresses' looks didn't matter as much as how fast they brought the drinks and how often they smiled. A little switch of the ass now and then didn't hurt business either. After a while, everything would be a big blur anyway. And the dance floor couldn't be too big since squeezing onto a crowded area and bumpin' and grindin' in the dark was "oh so mellow!"

The trio was on break when Clara and Scully walked into the Social Club. Heads turned in their direction as an Aretha Franklin record played on the jukebox.

Scully and Clara knew they were looking good! Scully had changed to a navy blue denim suit with a gold and blue print shirt. His dark blue platform shoes raised him above the crowd. Clara's black kiana dress hugged every curve in her body. A V-neckline ended at her navel with a sparkling rhinestone pin at the point of the V. Tonight she looked like her idol, Dorothy Dandridge. She didn't go for packed clubs but Scully was big shit in the Social Club and he wanted her with him.

Clara held Scully by the arm but stood slightly apart from him as if she felt herself slightly better than him and the other blacks in the club. She definitely had it all and she played the role. She struck a sexy pose for her admirers even though she didn't give a damn about them.

"You got it, daddy," yelled a tall thin customer as he greeted Scully with a hand slap.

"Naw, Blue," answered Scully, trying to be cool.

Scully turned to talk to a waitress who rubbed next to him as she passed. Blue moved closer to Clara and whispered in her ear.

"You oughta get rid of this nigger." His breath reeked of so much whiskey that Clara twisted her face in disgust and then said sharply,

"Honey, you can't handle it!"

Scully turned and laughed as Clara pushed Blue out of her way.

15

"She sho' turned your ass around!"

"Ain't no big thang," he snorted. "You can't last forever!"

Clara sensed trouble and reached for Scully's arm for security. Big Blue's woman watched with raised eyebrows and decided to make her way across the packed room and show him two could play that game. She was as slinky as a Siamese cat and she didn't give a damn. LuAnn switched her ass as she moved toward Scully and Clara.

"Hey, Scully," LuAnn slurred in a sultry voice as she ran her fingers across his neck.

Scully enjoyed this attention as his shoulder rubbed against her half bare breasts.

"Don't pay us no mind, Clara," she continued sarcastically.

"She don't mind, honey."

That's all LuAnn needed to hear. She turned Scully's face toward her and thrust her tongue in his mouth. Clara was seething.

"Relax," said Blue as he handed Clara a drink. "They don't mean no harm."

Clara pushed his arm out of her way, causing the iceless drink to spill, barely missing her expensive dress.

Blue mumbled to himself and pulled LuAnn away from Scully.

"C'mon, Scully," said Clara as she pushed her

way through the crowd and toward the bar, "this air's too stale for me!"

Scully followed slowly as if enjoying all the attention he was getting. LuAnn was known for fighting over men but Clara wasn't about to lower herself to fighting over any man, not even Scully.

All eyes were on them as they moved toward the bar. It wouldn't be Saturday night if there wasn't a fight.

Scully smiled and waved like a candidate running for office.

LuAnn wouldn't be outdone and trotted behind them. By the time Blue knew what was happening, LuAnn had caught up with Scully and Clara.

"You betta come off that shit, honey. Who do you think you are? Hollywood ain't come lookin' for you!"

Clara brushed her off.

"LuAnn, Harlem wouldn't think you fit enough to lay in its gutters!"

"Why—why, you bitch!" she sneered as Scully tried to calm her down.

"Anytime you're ready, Scully. You know where to find me." She stumbled away calling for Blue as the trio returned to the bandstand.

Already Clara was tired of the blacks. She reached the bar and leaned against the soft padding for relief. Scully was trying for a comeback as he

17

put his big muscular hands around her waist. But his touch pissed her off!

"No sense in waitin', Scully. If you want her, go on now! I'd do better at home anyway!"

"Ah, baby, you know I was just jokin' with her."

Clara didn't soften a bit, she just looked straight ahead at the mirror in front of her which was behind rows of liquor bottles.

Scully wasn't about to be ignored, especially in front of his partners.

Clara called to the bartender to bring her a Salty Dog.

"You must think you're Miss Ann!"

"Miss Ann, Miss Bessie Mae, they're all the same around here!" she answered loudly with her glass tipped.

Just as the bartender brought Scully his usual gin and tonic, a chubby light-skinned kid in his early twenties eased between him and the dude standing next to him at the bar.

"I think we got some business, man," the red dude said softly.

He caught Scully by surprise.

"Don't hand me no shit about business, man. I'm out with my lady. We'll deal later!"

It wasn't like Scully to start any trouble when he was clean. And he was definitely clean tonight!

By Bobbye B. Vance

Besides, he sensed Red was up tight about some cocaine he had said he would deliver and didn't. News was out that Red had turned police informer the week before because the mayor had ordered an investigation into dope traffic among city employees. Red was a fireman and there weren't that many blacks in that department. It was a soft job when there wasn't a fire and Red couldn't hack working in the hot, sweaty steel mill.

Scully usually got his supply around the time of the monthly board meeting at the mill. Once it was cut, he'd drop by the fire station and Red would deal with it from there. But Scully was tipped off and sensed trouble. So this last time, he didn't show up. The cops were closing in on Red and he wasn't coming through with the man they wanted. The deal had to go through tonight or it was all over for him!

"Look, Red, why don't—" Scully stopped talking when he saw Red move toward Clara who had turned away from the bar to watch the trio. Red moved even closer and before Clara knew what was happening, liquor was trickling down between her breasts.

"Hey, man, watch that shit!" yelled Scully.

"Forget it, Scully!" Clara said as she tried to control her anger.

Red mumbled a few words which Scully could

barely understand. The music blasted but it didn't
distract the attention from the bar. All eyes were
on Scully and Red. Before Red could raise his arm
to protect his face, Scully's fist landed with the
force of a brick. Red had all he could do to stay on
his feet but he was too weak and crashed into a
table as drinks spilled everywhere. The two dudes
sitting at the table moved just in time. Chicks were
screaming all over the place and blacks stumbled
over each other, tables, chairs, trying to get out of
the way.

Blood trickled from Red's eye. He got up slowly
as if defeated, but quickly picked up a wooden
chair and crashed it into Scully's groin as fast as a
bullet. He fell backwards against the bar as the pain
struck like lightning. He doubled with pain as Clara
screamed his name.

Clara had been pushed back in the crowd and
couldn't get through to Scully. No one seemed to
leave. They really didn't want to miss any of the
action. They just didn't want to get killed. LuAnn
staggered toward Scully as if to save him. But as he
pushed her out of the way, he ripped off the front
of her thin blouse, exposing her breasts. She gasped
with shock and tried in vain to cover herself from
the eyes of the gawking dudes.

Scully and Red kept tearing into each other with
all the fury and anger within them as other fights

20

broke out all over the room. Scully grabbed a nearby pool stick and drove it into the pit of Red's stomach.

"Ah, you bastard," Red groaned through clenched teeth as he rammed the pool stick back into Scully's side. They crashed into the pool table and fell to the hard floor, taking a chair with them. Again and again Scully's fist smashed into Red's battered body. Scully's eyes were puffy and his lips were swollen and strained with blood, but he was getting the best of Red.

The club was wild with confusion. Dudes were jamming back. Chicks were screaming and crying. Any second the sound of a gun firing a fatal bullet was expected. Instead, a police siren grew louder as it neared the entrance of the club.

The sound of doors being slammed forcefully was heard seconds before two white policemen rushed into the club with guns ready to kill a nigger.

"Okay, don't anyone move," warned the tallest cop whose hatred for black folks was written all over his red face. Silence swept through the room. It just wasn't Saturday night unless some poor black didn't have his head bashed in by a cop. Who would it be tonight?

Yanavitch had covered the Taft and Eleventh area for six years and had earned the reputation of being rough on blacks.

He had been acquitted of the murder of a black teenager in a robbery attempt two years earlier. Yanavitch patrolled the streets with only one thought in mind: keep the animals in their place. He had his chance again. But this time he called for the rookie to get re-inforcements. Perhaps, he thought there were too many nappy-headed big-eyed monkies for him to deal with.

Big J.A. didn't give a damn and moved swiftly toward Scully and Red who by this time lay bleeding on the hard wooden dance floor. There wasn't much fight left in them now. Red was hoping to put Scully in a trick because he figured Scully would probably make a deal with Big J.A. before the night was over.

Since it was obvious that he didn't have the stuff on him, he may have stashed it in the car.

As Scully staggered to his feet he sensed what was about to happen. He seldom stashed drugs in the car when Clara was with him but he had changed clothes at her house and hadn't bothered to go back to his rented room.

"What a dumb ass fool," he thought as he realized that the drugs would be found.

Clara was trembling as tears streaked her mascara. Her silk dark hair was slowly sliding from the top of her head. No one comforted her. No one dared to move. She started toward Scully but stopped when he shook his battered head.

Within a split second Clara could see her career crumble in the Social Club of Gary, Indiana. She had to make a move! It was leave Gary now or else forget about being a movie star.

3 . . .

It was after four o'clock a.m. when the cab stopped in front of Clara's apartment building. The street was quiet as the blackness of night blanketed the city. Saturday was over and with it went Clara's past.

Her apartment was lonely without Scully. She found herself telling her aching body to move slowly to her bedroom. The chenile bedspread was untouched. It would have been so much better to see Scully's naked body lying there. She wanted to pass out but instead she leaned against the bedroom door as her tired eyes gazed at the life-sized posters of herself that plastered the walls.

By Bobbye B. Vance

The tears flowed like water now. No one could see her release the ache she had carried in the pit of her stomach. She could only think of the few minutes they had spent together at the police station.

"What are they gonna do to you, Scully?" she asked nervously.

"They just gonna try and get me on some jive ass charges, baby," he had said.

"Honey, this is no life for you! I can make it in Hollywood. As soon as you get out let's go. I got money saved and—"

"Naw, Clara, this life right here is good enough for me. You know what I mean? Now, I'm gonna get out. Nothin' these fuckin' cops or that son-of-bitch Red can do 'bout it. Baby, you ain't mixed up in this no way. So you don't have to go no place!"

He still wanted her to be there, she thought as she pushed herself away from the door and toward the closet. Her red suitcase was light but in a few minutes it would be stuffed with as much as it could carry.

She pulled open her dresser drawers with more confidence now. She was going to get out before Scully called and weakened her again.

By the time she got herself together, it was bright enough to walk the streets.

25

Clara walked briskly to Broadway as the summer's sun tried to peak through the gray sky.

She still felt drained from all that went down the night before. Scully, the club, the racist cops, drugs, and a life without a future added to a bad scene. At least she had a way out. At least she had enough determination and belief in herself to get the hell out while she could. So she sat on the wooden bench in her tight red suit with hopes of stardom sparkling in her dark brown eyes.

Her deep thoughts were broken as a blue Chevy pulled up to a stop.

"Can I give ya a lift, sister?" smiled the middle-aged black man with graying hair in a well meaning voice.

"Thanks, brother. But I'm going a mighty long way."

He winked his eye as if understanding what she meant and drove off in the opposite direction.

She checked her watch for the time and thought the bus would arrive in a few minutes.

The city was beginning to stir as light traffic moved slowly along the street. Most blacks were still asleep, while the faithful few would be rising soon to praise the Lord and ask forgiveness for their usual weekly sins!

A shock went through Clara as a Ford with three different paint jobs screeched to a hault in front of her. It bucked like a horse as its hillbilly driver grinned with tobacco-stained teeth as he peered through the window.

"Hop in, sugah!" beamed the pussy-hungry pervert.

"Clara's eyes narrowed with disgust as her lips tightened with fury. Who did this bastard think he was?

"L-l-look, I got money!" His hands shook as he pulled two crumpled five dollar bills out of his bib overalls, and flipped down the door handle, pushing the door open for her to get in.

Waiting for busses pissed Clara off! She could always count on some cracker trying to pick her up. Then she'd have to act like a nigger to get rid of them!

"Stick it up your ass and give yourself a thrill, motherfucker!" she sneered as the veins in her neck popped in view.

The hillbilly drove away cussing his ass off! The car bucked again as the door on the passenger's side flapped with the force of the sudden takeoff.

"Hmph! It's a damn shame people like that don't ever get lynched!"

Clara was so uptight that she didn't notice the motorcycle cop sitting patiently across the street in front of the bank. His arms were folded calmly as his leather gloves quietly patted his chubby arms that were somewhere beneath a heavy leather jacket.

His crash helmet and dark shades didn't hide the vibes that Clara was beginning to feel.

"Oh, shit! Here we go again!"

Ripley moved like the typical Southern redneck cop. His hatred for niggers was as deep as Yanavitch's.

Smack, smack, smack! went the night stick as he hit it into the palm of his leather gloves.

That could be upside my head, if I don't get the hell out of here! Clara thought.

Traffic seemed to have disappeared and only the sounds of distant cars broke the silence.

His walk made her uneasy. The closer he came, the louder the sound of the night stick rang in her ears. His legs were so big she could hear his thighs rubbing together.

Something inside her told her to get up fast in case the bus came down the street. She tried to be cool as the redneck planted his big boots firmly in front of the curb.

A nearby parking meter was her source of comfort and support.

"What's wrong, girlie? Ain't the price right?"

"Wha-What? Oh, I'm just waiting for the bus," she sputtered as she looked down the long street.

Ripley shook his head in disbelief as he looked

up at Clara. As far as he was concerned she was just another black hooker all painted up like Christmas and trying to turn a Sunday morning trick.

"You look mo' like you're waitin' for a traveling salesman's convention!"

Clara's jaws got tight again!

"Now, wait just a—" she blurted out with her hands on her hips.

"Hold it, girlie. I think you better to be waitin'!" he interrupted. "Jus' sit right there on the bench next to that bag and don't move, lessin' that bus comes or else I'll put your ass where the only trick you'll turn'll be behind bars, ya' heah!"

Clara had to bite her lip with all the strength she had to keep from saying the wrong thing. She moved toward the bench and sat in her most lady-like position.

"Now, that's more like it," he grinned. "I'm gonna sit right over on my bike and keep a mighty close eye on ya!"

He turned and hurried back to his bike and sat with arms crossed like a pompous Buddha.

She sighed in relief and tried to pull herself together. Frustration was wearing her down and she couldn't hack it much longer.

No sooner had the cop settled down when a new foreign sports car drove up and stopped in front of Clara. The motor ran loud, causing the handsome young white driver to talk loudly.

"How about a ride. That bus won't be here for about an hour."

Clara's eyes fleeted back and forth from the redneck cop to the clean cut white guy in front of her. She had to make a decision fast because Ripley dismounted his bike and was heading her way.

"No, no. Just get away before I—" she stopped as Ripley entered the middle of the street.

The driver glanced at the cop and could sense what was about to happen.

"Look, I'm going to the coast so I can drop you off anywhere between—"

"You got a deal," she interrupted as she grabbed her suitcase and threw it on the luggage rack in the back."

The tires screeched loudly as they whizzed past Ripley who yanked off his helmet and pounded it disgustedly with his fist.

"Let's split, mister," ordered Clara as she peered through the trailing cloud of smoke. Officer Ripley was boiling as the two headed out of sight.

Clara nestled back into the soft gray leather seat of the silver Porsche as they raced along the interstate.

They both laughed about the flustered cop left behind.

By the time it hit Clara that she didn't know

anything about this white dude sitting next to her, she was outside Gary.

"Hey, I'm Clara Brown," she smiled warmly.

"And I'm Tony." He returned her smile.

"Man, what a relief," she sighed. "Did you see that bulldog's face?"

They both roared with laughter as the tension wore off.

Tony's light brown hair flopped slightly above his forehead. He looked as if he could be about her height if she didn't wear shoes. His tan complexion made it obvious that he had spent a lot of time in the sun.

Clara kind of liked his looks. She checked out his muscular arms and chest through his white sheer casual shirt and his slim thighs that were hidden beneath his beige slacks.

This might be a good change after all, thought Clara as she reached over to light his menthol cigarette.

"Thanks," he puffed, causing his chest to rise and fall smoothly. "I bet you're on your way to Hollywood to become a big star."

"Hey," she remarked suddenly, "how'd you guess?"

"Well, a beauty like you can't waste her time in a place like Gary."

"Yeah, I've had it here. I went to college and

31

majored in drama but all I ended up doing was work with a group of kids. Oh, I'm not knocking that. You know. It's just that people just didn't dig what we were into at the level we were into it. Know what I mean?"

Tony nodded.

"Well," she continued, "We had a damn good theatre group. We were rehearsing to do 'Anna Lucasta' . . . she paused . . . that is until I just left. Like up till today."

"Don't you think they'll be let down?" Tony asked.

"Sure. Pissed off would be a better way to say it," she assured him. "But, man, there were so many things about to go down funky that if I didn't get out, some of those well-meaning white folks who have helped finance our program would have quit as soon as my name had the slightest bad odor. So, it was best. There's always someone to pick up where you left off. The hardest thing to deal with is picking yourself up when the chips are down. And I do mean down!"

There was nothing but sun beating down on their heads as they drove along the interstate. The farther west they travelled, the hotter it would get but that didn't matter. The air was cool, the ride was free, and the chauffeur was white! And Clara Brown was on her way!

Clara went on and on about her self, her plans and her dreams. She didn't mention Scully by name, but she talked about the man she loved and how his values just messed up her future. So she had to cut him loose.

Tony didn't talk much about himself. Instead he kept pitching questions at Clara.

"How do you plan to live on the West Coast?" he asked.

"Oh, I've been saving for this day," she assured him. "Besides, it won't take me long to get in somebody's movie."

"I hear you can make a quick killing but it's rough to make that day to day thing," he quickly responded, casting doubt on her chances.

"Say, maybe you should be my manager!" she suggested with a big smile.

"Naw," he shook his head, "I just told you why that life's not for me. I have to be sure of where I'm going, and sleeping, everyday. I've never been much for taking chances." He turned and winked at Clara. "Except when a pretty woman looks like she needs my help."

Right on! thought Clara. It did her good to hear someone talk some sense around her head! She figured that the ride might not be so bad after all. But time would tell. They stopped to eat along the way and spent nights in Howard Johnson Motels.

BLACK STARLET

She had feared the first night. Being so far away
from anyone she knew meant that she couldn't yell
for help. But Tony casually said that he'd pay for
their separate rooms which set her mind at ease.
Clara Brown had found herself a gentleman!

• • • 4

It was a rainy day when they rolled into Las Vegas, but the hot morning sun would soon dry the streets. Tony nudged Clara as they cruised down.

"So, this is Vegas," yawned Clara as they stopped for a light at Riviera Boulevard.

"Check out that merry-go-round in front of Circus Circus!" she pointed. "Man, I'm like a kid when I see all this. Who'd think of doing something like that?"

"Anything to get your money, Clara, anything!"

Even the chapels on Las Vegas Boulevard excited Clara. But marriage was the last thing on her mind!

The marquees of the Stardust, the MGM Grand and the Hilton named top acts.

"Maybe we can catch Red Foxx at the Hilton?" Tony suggested.

"It's okay with me, but let's not spend too much time here. It'd really piss me off if I got this far and lost my money in the slot machines or something!"

"Humph! I wouldn't let anything happen to you, Miss Star," laughed Tony.

"Right now I want to get out of these sticky clothes."

"Why don't we get a room in a small hotel off Carson and spend a few hours in some club. I'll check on tickets to see Red Foxx tonight."

Clara didn't hear Tony say anything about two rooms. And as they drove into the light stucco motel she was convinced. He had been good to her so maybe it was time to be good to him. She'd screwed other men who hadn't done half as much for her!

The room overlooked the mountains that formed an impressive backdrop behind the swaying green palms and the desert's light sand. Clara was used to lots of trees and cooler air, but it was a change to really see miles and miles of cotton-like clouds sailing across the sky.

Tony brought the bags in as Clara collapsed on

the bed.

"How would you like for me to get some food for us and bring it back?" asked Tony.

"That's fine. In the meantime, I'll take a quick shower and change." Clara pulled herself off the powder blue bedspread and walked toward the window to open the white venetian blinds. She changed her mind and peeled off her clothes as her feet slid through the shag carpet to the white tiled bathroom.

Within seconds the spray from the hot shower was pounding away at her body, washing the grubby feeling she had picked up from travelling the last eight hours.

She didn't hear the clicking of the key as it entered the keyhole in the door of the motel room and she didn't hear the slow turn of the doorknob of the bathroom. Locking the door had slipped her mind!

The white figure creeped into the small bathroom. Hidden faintly by the steam and separated mainly by the shower curtain, he waited for her to turn off the shower.

Clara reached forward to stop the fierce flow of water and quickly pushed back the curtain.

"Ahh!" she gasped in fright. "What the hell is this?"

The shower curtain was wrapped around her

now to hide her nakedness.

Tony let out a roar of laughter as he handed her a towel.

"I'm not much for practical jokes, man! Especially in the bathroom!"

"Sorry, Clara, I didn't mean to scare you. My car wouldn't start so I thought I'd come back and suggest catching a cab someplace close by."

Clara's heart was still racing but she wasn't going to let this white man know that he had scared the hell out of her!

"Oh, ok," she said disappointedly. "It really doesn't matter. I'm not too hungry right this minute. Anyway, take a look in my suitcase and get my red print housecoat, will you?"

Tony searched through the suitcase until his hands touched the soft nylon material with its satin trim.

"Just hand it to me," she ordered. "We can talk when I come out."

"Alright, Miss Hollywood," he surrendered. "I'm going to pour us a drink to . . ."

"Easy for me. It's still too early. Besides, I'm not really a drinker," she confessed.

"Clara Brown, I've learned a lot about you these last few days."

"Like what?" she asked through the closed door.

"Like you're warm, ambitious, intelligent . . . and trusting."

"Wow! You're some dude!" she laughed. "You must be tryin' for the jackpot, 'cause you just came pretty close to knowin' the re-e-al me!"

Clara's nakedness beneath the red housecoat caught his eyes!

"Wow!" he whistled. "Just sit right down on this soft bed and I'll bring your drink, madam."

There was little room for anything else on the small walnut night stand between the two double beds, but Tony squeezed the small ice bucket aside and fixed Clara's drink.

"I hope this is just right."

"I'm not much of a Scotch drinker, but let me taste it." She could taste more Scotch than water.

"Ugh," she said, with the corners of her mouth turned down. "Go easy on me, man!"

"Here, let me have the glass. I'll go in the bathroom and add more water."

When he returned, he walked toward the blinds and blocked out the early morning hot Vegas sun.

"O-o-o-we-e-w! I guess I have to keep fanning to cool off this fire racing down my stomach!"

"Aw, c'mon. It's not that bad!" he assured her. "Here, this will cool you down."

Clara watched the drink change to a lighter gold color. Putting it to her lips was the test.

"Now, that's more like it!" she assured him. A few sips more was all she needed.

Tony told her a few simple dirty white jokes that made her giggle.

"Oh, shit," she laughed. "How can you stand those dry jokes. Why Scully could . . ."

Mentioning his name brought a tower of memories crashing down around her.

"Scully," she whispered as tears rolled from the corners of her eyes. Tony's thigh rubbed next to hers as he sat down in the quiet room.

"Hey, where's the bubbling Clara Brown I met a few days ago?"

The urge for a man's soft touch was rising inside her.

Tony kissed her soft cheek and she closed her eyes to block out what would follow.

Only the rustling of clothes and the groans of passion could be heard above the city street.

His hot sweaty body didn't phase her in the least. Even knowing that she was going to get screwed by a white man didn't shock her. She just needed a man and she needed one now!

They were wrapped around each other as the bedspread followed their path. Tony's hot lips sucked her pointed nipples as fingers combed through her hair. The more he grinded his white body into hers, the harder he got. Louder and

40

louder he breathed as Clara's movements teased him. Suddenly her thighs slapped tightly together and her body stiffened. He was puzzled. Why was she turning him off? Her fists pounded against his flesh in anger.

"Don't, Tony," she demanded.

"What the fuck is wrong with you?" he asked as his hands squeezed her hips. His force felt as if her bones would crush.

"Just don't touch me! Don't put your stinkin' hands on me!"

He smelled white and that was enough to turn her stomach. She tried to fight him off as they wrestled violently.

"Why you black bitch," he sneered.

Whack! His open hand slapped her face. *Whack! whack! whack!* He slapped her until his hand was red!

"No, no!" she screamed in terror. "Don't hit me! Don't hit me!"

"Those tears don't do nothin' to me, bitch. You're gonna get fucked whether you like it or not. So you may as well lay back and enjoy it!"

She was fighting for her life but the blows to the face and body were wearing her down. She fought him off as long as she could, but his strength was too much for her thin frame. She was desperate as she bit into his shoulder. She held on until she

41

tasted drops of blood.

"Goddammit!" he roared as his fist landed on her chin. Clara was motionless. She didn't feel him push her thighs apart. But he was in her now, releasing all his fiery white hatred.

Jolts of pain ran like crazy through her battered body when her bruised eyes finally opened.

"Oh, Christ!" she said as she looked at the cream colored walls. "Everything is all blurred!"

She placed her hand between her legs and the pain she felt under her soft hands went deeper at her touch.

She wanted to piss but the thought of worse pain convinced her to tighten up.

"Oh," she moaned as she rocked painfully on the rumpled sheets. "Somebody help me, somebody help me!" But her voice was too faint to be heard.

She wanted to give in but a voice inside kept talking to her until she was on her wobbly feet and dragging herself to the bathroom.

Flick went the light switch, only to expose a messed up black chick. Her body was a patchwork of bruises. The sight caused her to tremble, but that same voice told her to get herself together and get the hell out of there!

"My money," she thought as she hobbled out of the bathroom toward her pocketbook.

She rummaged through it, hoping desperately to find her wallet. She shook it frantically, then ripped it apart in anger.

"That honky! That fuckin' honky!" she screamed at the top of her lungs. Her legs collapsed and she landed on the floor in tears, scattering everything in her bag in front of her.

Clara knew that the cops wouldn't believe her story so the wisest thing to do would be to pull herself together and get out fast! She'd have to thumb, but she knew damn well that she would never again think about catching a ride from a white bastard!

5 . . .

It was a sweltering one hundred and fifteen degrees when Clara slowly reached the entrance ramp of Interstate Fifteen.

Neither the intense heat nor her aching body sapped her energy. The pain she felt from Tony's fists wasn't enough to keep her from Hollywood!

The thought of thumbing again was unpleasant but she had no choice. Perhaps she'd be a little choosy this time. Riding with white folks was out! There was no guarantee that someone black would treat her any better but, at least, she'd like to think so.

Twenty-five hot minutes had passed before her first offer. Two white stringy blond teenaged boys pulled up in a late model car but Clara wouldn't look their way.

Her tight black pants and jacket would have attracted pink people, but black folks were all she wanted to see.

She pulled her wide black hat over her face to hide the bruises Tony had planted on her. But it was another ten minutes before anyone stopped. Most looked into her face and realized that picking her up might mean more trouble than she was worth.

"I'm not gonna get up tight," she thought out loud. "I probably wouldn't pick me up either!"

Weakness had just about conquered her when a black 1954 pick-up truck chugged pass. It stopped about ten feet in front of her and then rocked backwards until it was directly in front of her.

An elderly chubby couple peered at Clara with warm smiles. Both looked to be in their late fifties. The man's eyes were deeply set and his white hair was a sharp contrast to his round brown face. The blue bib overall he wore over a red plaid shirt showed months of wear. Next to him calmly sat a plump woman with clear smooth light brown skin. Her hair was thin but it was still dark brown. Her breasts were so big that the buttons down the front of her green housedress looked as if they would pop any minute. Rolls of fat covered her arms but no wrinkles could be found.

"Can we give you a lift, Miss," said the round-faced, middle-aged black woman.

Clara didn't even bother to answer. Her face was alive again! A sudden burst of hope ran through her body as she pulled down the handle of the black dented-in door. She was so excited that she almost forgot her bag.

"I'm Johnnye Mae Johnson and this here is my husband. We don't usually pick up folks but you look like you had a rough time of it. So I guess the Lawd gave us an extra nudge."

Clara could see the warmth in their eyes and knew that they were just kind folks. They were both fat but she was able to squeeze into a comfortable spot.

The truck drove off slowly and surprisingly picked up speed as it rocked along.

"I really have had a rough time, but I know things will be a lot better. Are you going to L.A.?"

"Yes'm," nodded the gray-haired man. "We from Alabama but Mama, here, got relatives in Los Angeles. Things got so bad on the farm this year, we decided to leave. It ain't easy for us ole' folks to pick up but life ain't no good for black folks there, 'specially if you sharecroppin'. We thought we'd stop in Vegas. Might never get this way again . Ole' Nellie is a might slow, but she'll get us to

Califo'na."

Clara felt as if she needed to pour out her troubles and she did.

The ride was bumpy but pleasant as they talked on and on.

Darkness covered the city as the truck creeped onto the freeway. Clara had fallen asleep from exhaustion.

"Miss Clara, Miss Clara," nudged Mrs. Johnson, "we almost there!"

Clara's eyes opened slowly.

"Oh, you can let me off anywhere near Hollywood and Vine," she answered sleepily.

"This ain't no time to be on the streets. Besides, my sister got room for you. After a good ole' down home breakfast of grits, eggs, homemade sausage and biscuits with syrup, you'll feel betta' and look betta', too," said Mrs. Johnson.

She was right, thought Clara. Besides, she didn't have a dime.

It wasn't until early morning that Clara got her first look at the explosive community of Watts. The hazy sky hovered over the calm neighborhood as the old truck rocked across the railroad on Wilmington.

Standing strong and tall were the mosaic Watts Towers that reached almost one hundred feet into the air.

"Can you see those towers?" Clara asked the Johnsons as she pointed to her left.

"One black man did that! Can you imagine what all our people put together could do?"

The elderly couple nodded but Clara could tell by their deep set eyes that they had come to California for a peaceful life and not to fight any more battles.

As they slowly approached the Watts Neighborhood Center, Clara read the bright bold word on the tall beige stucco building. A black silhouette painted in red, black and green drew their attention.

"MAFUNDI," Clara read. "That means 'craftsmen'."

"Miss Clara, you sure you ain't no teacher," laughed Mr. Johnson as his stomach shook beneath his rumpled blue denim overalls.

"No, that's not my thing, I'm an actress. Besides, you gotta know a lot about your own people these days. I learned that in the streets, not in schools!"

Mrs. Johnson quickly changed the subject.

"This don't look as bad as they made it look on the TV when they had all that burnin'."

Her head went from left to right as they drove up 103rd Street.

"Just look at all those pretty stucco houses!

By Bobbye B. Vance

Pinks, blues, beiges . . . and looka yonda' at all that black iron on that house," she pointed across Clara who was sitting next to the door.

"Yup," answered Mr. Johnson, "them watcha call 'ems Spanish tile. Yup, Spanish tile roofs are sump'in different. You see 'em all over the place."

"Well, this street looks pretty clean. Flowers in the yards, houses a little too close, though," remarked Clara. "Back there in those empty lots was probably part of what was burned down. At least that looks like what I saw on television."

"Humph!" grumbled Mr. Johnson, "White folks only let you see what they want you to see. They always makin' us look so bad on the television, showin' the worse houses and people. They do the same in them movies, too. Why, to hear them tell it we ain't got no nice places to live in and no good jobs. They keep everyone thinkin' all we do is lay around, make babies, and shoot the baby's mama 'cuz she looks at another nigger! I tell you, po' white trash is worse than our people will ever be! But they don't show them that much in the movies."

His lips closed tightly with anger.

"Lawd-a-mercy, Papa! You ain't never talked like that befo'," said Mrs. Johnson with a puzzled look.

"That's 'cuz I ain't down home no mo'!" he

49

answered with force. "Them swayin' palm trees
and pretty skies, even if it is smoggy, makes a man
feel free! Havin' another chance!" He sucked in a
deep breath of air. "You know what I mean, Miss
Clara?"

His fiery remarks were still ringing in her ears.
Perhaps, there was some spirit left in the old man
after all.

"Miss Clara?" he called again.

"Oh-h-h," she stuttered, "yes, Mr. Johnson. I
know exactly where you're comin' from! Exactly!" she answered assuredly.

The ride along the Harbor Freeway was quiet
with only small talk about the forest green land-
scaping along the freeway. Traffic was thickening
but the truck refused to overheat as it kept up with
Bentleys, Mercedes and Jaguars which crowded the
lanes.

What was ahead of Clara now that she was
heading toward Hollywood? Los Angeles spread
out four hundred and fifty-four miles and she
planned to be around a long time to see as much of
it as she could.

When they finally reached the Hollywood
Freeway, Clara pulled a city map out of her cluttered pocketbook. The paper rattled loudly as she
attempted to find Hollywood and Vine.

"Keep going until we come to a Hollywood

Boulevard exit," she instructed.

"We sure wish you'd stay with m' sista-in-law, Miss Clara," said Mrs. Johnson warmly. Her eyes never left the road. "She could squeeze you in for a while. You don't eat much and you as thin as a rail so you won't take up much room."

"Thanks, ma'am. But I really got to get a job and a place of my own. You have been too kind already. My bruises are just about gone on my face. At least, I can cover them with make-up now. I know I'm gonna be a star and I really feel I'll get my big break real soon!" she said with a burst of confidence.

Clara was becoming excited at the thought of getting a big break. Her finger moved across the city map as she attempted to give Mr. Johnson directions. Traffic was picking up as early morning workers headed toward the downtown Hollywood area.

"Now, I don't want you to have to make a turn at the last minute, Mr. Johnson, so I'll let you know when we get close."

Mr Johnson's big wrinkled hands slid up and down along the outer edges of the steering wheel. He wasn't used to Los Angeles traffic. No one was! He was getting nervous, but followed Clara's directions.

They rode and rode until finally, the street sign

51

saying Vine Street caught Clara's eye.

"Oh, look! Right here at the light!" she pointed to the sign in front of the American Airlines information center.

"So, this is it!" she smiled with excitement. "Hollywood and Vine!"

"Don't see nothin' much around here 'cept a lot of folks lookin' like they belong in the circus or at some costume party!" laughed Mr. Johnson.

"Yes, Lawd. You got that right, Papa," added Mrs. Johnson. "Look at 'em all sparklin', wild-lookin' outfits—whole lotta glitter, that's for sure. If this is how ya' get in the movies, Miss Clara, maybe you betta put on somethin' that looks like tinsel so folk'll look at ya!"

It was the first time all three had laughed so loudly.

"Don't get me wrong. That black suit be fittin' you. Showin' all your 'uh curves, but . . ."

"But," interrupted Clara, "don't worry, ma'am. I'll get discovered. Nobody does any more than look at these freaky people!"

Mrs. Johnson wasn't convinced but nodded her head in agreement.

"Wait," ordered Clara, "Let me off right here."

Mr. Johnson steered the truck to the curb in front of Grauman's Chinese Theatre.

Clara looked warmly into the gentle eyes of the

old couple. Their faces showed the sadness they felt as Clara said goodbye.

"I just don't know how to thank you. You've been so good to me. When you picked me up in Vegas, I felt pretty discouraged, but after meeting and talking with both of you I know I can make it. And Mr. Johnson, when I do, I hope after I'm a big star that I find a man just like you. You know, you still have a lot of fire and guts left in you."

Mr. Johnson had the nerve to blush!

"Why, that's right nice of you, Miss Clara."

Clara hopped up and pulled her suitcase over the side panel of the back. Her slender fingers spread around Mrs. Johnson's chubby brown hand which was extended over the window of the door.

"Take this, chile," Mrs. Johnson insisted.

"No, I can't do that. I can't take your money, ma'am. You've both done enough for me. And your sister-in-law, too." She patted Mrs. Johnson's hand.

Mrs. Johnson's smile was enough to let Clara know that she understood.

"God be with you, Miss Clara. God be with you," prayed Mrs. Johnson.

6. . .

Then the first warm people Clara had met in weeks were moving down Hollywood Boulevard and out of sight. She had wanted to say the same for them, but was too filled up with tears to say it. Perhaps they understood by the well-meaning look in her eyes.

"So, this is Grauman's Chinese Theatre!" she said as her eyes widened with excitement.

Clara had read about the star-studded premieres that had been held at this typically Chinese building. Its huge gray structure was trimmed in red with black iron steeples.

Two smaller buildings in front of the theatre were crowded with souvenir seekers and the word "CHINESE" could be seen in bright, bold letters on top of each building. A red metal arched canopy covered the famous entrance as camera-carrying tourists walked around it and in the courtyard between the theatre and the souvenir shops, gawking at the signatures, foot and hand prints of stars like Red Skelton, Shirley Temple, Sidney Poitier, Jean Harlow, and Clark Gable. Jimmy Durante had even put his big nose in the once wet cement!

The names of Academy Award-winning movies and artists appeared in a display window as people pointed to their favorite movie or actor.

"It's a damn shame more black actors and actresses don't get the credit they deserve!" squawked Clara as she knelt next to Sidney Poitier's signature.

"Well, I'll change all that!" she said confidently as she walked toward Vine Street. The sidewalks on Hollywood were lined with the names of famous stars.

"Marilyn Monroe's star! She *made* herself a name," Clara remarked as she stepped on the word "MARILYN."

Finding a job wouldn't be easy but Clara knew the only way to make it was to think positively. She was getting caught up in the Hollywood air.

"Maybe someone will discover me right now!" she hoped as she smiled at every white man who

passed, wishing that one might be a director looking for a pretty black face.

"How about a job, girlie," smiled a red-faced
blond man.

Clara looked at the figure of a topless dancer on
the window behind the man.

"You can make a good deal of money here. A
looker like you can catch plenty on the side!"

Clara's stomach turned as she thought about the
last white motherfucker who called himself helping
her.

"You know, I can co-operate. Yup, we should
team up," he said with a dirty grin as he greedily
eyed her full breasts.

"Sorry, Big Boy, try your luck with someone
else. You ain't my color or type!" she snapped
sarcastically and turned, switching her ass as she
passed.

He quickly mumbled something back at her but
a tour bus headed toward the Chinese Theatre
drowned his words.

Clara walked a complete block, asking for a job
in every shop, store and restaurant. It was useless.
But her legs would give out before her determination. The weight of her suitcase was wearing her
down as the noon sun pressed through her tight
black outfit like a hot iron.

She was facing Grauman's Theatre again when

56

By Bobbye B. Vance

she noticed a dry cleaners. She walked toward the cleaners and pressed her nose against the hot window. The counter was cluttered with rumpled laundry and a short stocky man was pitching a fit. He stopped the moment Clara walked through the door. Beads of sweat were dripping down her forehead and her curly hair was frizzled as it soaked up the sweat.

"Ya look like ya need a little dry cleanin', lady."

"What I need is a job," she answered tiredly.

"You got it! I'm Sam Spear and my best worker just quit! Howd'ya like that! Just up and quit!" he roared.

A typical Jew, thought Clara as she watched Sam wave his hands wildly in the air. His balding head wasn't as noticeable as his hooked nose that curved below his top lip. All the Jews she had known worked the hell out of black folks and paid low wages. But she needed a job and it didn't matter if he was South African! A job meant money!

"Just show me where to put my bag!" Clara smiled.

"Put it behind the counter and follow me. Now the first lesson is to work fast, hear me? Work fast! All the slobs in L.A. want their fuckin' pants at the same time and I gotta give 'em their fuckin' pants at the same time . . ."

57

Sam had a habit of nervously pulling his suspenders. The stinging sensations probably gave him a cheap thrill.

"Follow me," he said as he motioned toward the congested cleaning area in the back of the shop. Rows of clothes hung from overhead racks. Sam pushed the cellophane covered garments aside as if making a path through the deepest jungle. Clara followed like a slave being led to slaughter. Once through the jungle of clothes, Clara found herself in the middle of Sam Spear's gold mine. Four pressure machines were in operation while a fifth waited for Clara. A washing machine in a corner near a small window was sudsing away while an elderly frail black man sorted out the next load. Overhead racks lined with coat hangers and some clothes were everywhere.

Clara tried to step over scattered hangers that covered the floor as she followed Sam toward the empty pressure machine.

"Oh, by the way," he stopped abruptly, "this here is Joyce."

Clara smiled at the young brunette who appeared to be about twenty-five years old.

"Now don't fuck around, young lady! Ya keep ya' job as long as you keep up with the work. Ya gotta work fast, fast, fast!! Now, get to it!" he shook his finger in the direction of the full wagon bin of clothes next to a press.

He walked away complaining out loud and left Clara to figure out how to operate the heavy press machine.

Clara looked dumbfoundedly at the task before her but rolled up her sleeves and began to work. She picked up a wrinkled pair of gray trousers from the bin and quickly began pressing. The hood of the presser took a lot of force to bring down, but Clara held on tightly and did her thing. She knew that there wasn't any way to let her know when it was time to lift the hood. It was all a matter of using her own judgement. She felt confident as clouds of steam smacked her in the face. She looked over at Joyce. She was as calm as a cucumber. The heat of the machine seemed to have passed right over her.

Just then Clara's machine began to balk, causing Clara's eyes to widen in fright. Steam poured all around her as she pulled at the handle. Nothing happened and Clara shook the top handle as panic ran through her body.

"Aw, shit, I'm 'bout to put a hole right in my first pair of pants!" she yelled nervously.

"Just put your foot on the pedal, honey. Just put your foot on the pedal," Joyce answered calmly as she smoothed a freshly pressed pair of pants.

Clara pressed the pedal just in time. The hood flew up, leaving a neatly pressed pant leg. Clara sighed with relief as she mopped her sweaty forehead.

"What you gotta learn, honey, is that you let the machine do the work," remarked Joyce as Clara watched her press another pair of pants.

"I think I've got it now," Clara answered with a little more assurance. "But you're so damn calm about the whole thing. The heat from the machines don't even seem to bother you. How come?" Clara asked as she began pressing.

"Humph, it doesn't take long when you're hungry and need to keep a job."

Both girls smiled in agreement.

"You're new in town, aren't you?"

"Hey, is it that noticeable?" Clara asked.

"Well, this is usually where everyone comes when they hit L.A. Some are lucky enough to move up but some . . ."

"Having a social hour?" Sam interrupted with his hooked nose. "Remember, ladies," he pleaded as his chubby body shook, "all the slobs are waiting." He popped his suspenders and walked toward the front of the cleaners.

"He'll be on our necks every second. That man would work the hell out of his own mother if it meant bringin' in an extra dollar," grumbled Joyce.

"That's a Jew for ya'!" remarked Clara. "But, he's making the money and that's the name of the game. The whole thing is that we gotta suffer for it. But I don't plan to be here long . . ."

"I know," Joyce interrupted as she continued pressing. "You're here to put your name in lights. To be Hollywood's newest and hottest black beauty."

"I got talent," Clara snapped. She didn't want this white chick to think she was capitalizing on the rush for black females.

"Hold on, honey! I'm not for any causes. So, don't get me wrong. If you say you got talent, I believe you. But, if you've looked at yourself well enough lately, you'll see you're a good looker, too—once that eye clears up."

Clara quickly placed her hand over her bruised cheek.

"I didn't think it was still noticeable."

"Not really. Just traces. It'll be gone tomorrow."

"Tomorrow? Tomorrow? What's this about tomorrow?" Sam interrupted in fury. "Today! Today, ladies! All I want to hear is *'Pssssst! Pssssst!'* Ya got that? *'Psssst! Psssst!'* That's the loveliest sound in the world!"

A simple smile appeared on his face as he dumped a load of clothes into the bin and then beamed at Clara.

When he was out of sight Clara turned to Joyce and whispered.

"If he's that much in love with the damn machines, he probably screws 'em late at night!"

Fortunately, their laughter wasn't as loud as the steam pouring out of the machines.

It was a long hard day for Clara. But when it ended, she had a job, a friend, and a place to stay.

Joyce's apartment was off Hollywood and only a ten minute walk from the cleaners. The two-story pink stucco building was alive with plants on the porches and swaying palm trees in the yard. Having two floors made her feel as if she was in a house and less cramped.

Clara looked up just as the sun hid behind a puffy blue cloud.

"Does it always get this cool at night?"

"Yeah, it sure does. But you'll get use to it."

They walked up the stairs, loaded down with groceries and Clara's red suitcase. Joyce placed her grocery bag on the cement step and fumbled for her key. Once inside, both girls practically collapsed from exhaustion.

"Look, let's put this food away and get ourselves together."

"Just what do you have planned?" Clara asked.

"Nothing special. But, if you want to be a star,

you've got to hang out in the right places."

Clara looked around the narrow foyer which led to a living room with dark wooden beams and a bright colored Mexican rug over the dark floor. Studded walls were everywhere, giving the apartment a typically Mexican look. The furniture was typically Goodwill. But Joyce had added enough bright colors of red, orange, green, and gold to give the furniture more class then it had ever known.

Movie posters of Joyce in her short-lived career covered one wall in the living room.

A dining room and small pantry separated the kitchen, which overlooked a redwood fence and the living room. Boston ferns, spider plants, and split-leaf begonia's added a fresh outdoor feeling to an otherwise stiff look.

Movie fan magazines were stacked to the hilt next to the Victorian sofa, while *Variety* and *The Hollywood Reporter* were thrown around at will.

Clara sighed in relief as she plopped her bag of groceries on the kitchen table.

"It's taken me a long time to get here. I thought I'd never make it."

She leaned against the edge of the kitchen sink and told her story while Joyce put away the groceries.

"I'd say you've been fucked over enough," said Joyce once Clara was finished.

"You're damn right! And I hope that's the end of it, but I just know people are going to treat me much better. Things have been going great so far."

Joyce stopped short and put her hand on Clara's shoulder.

"Honey, I hope you really make it. You've got more of what it takes than I had." She took a beer out of the refrigerator and slumped into the kitchen chair. After taking a few swigs, she rubbed her breasts roughly.

"When I came here I knew Hollywood was waiting for me. Why, you couldn't tell me any different."

"You've got the looks," Clara assured her.

"Bullshit! I had about an inch of talent and minus five inches of sex drive. Screwin' every producer in town just wasn't my thing. But I did make a few features as you can see," bragged Joyce as she pointed to the skin flicks and horror posters on the walls.

"Well, why'd ya stay?" asked Clara.

"And go back home to Oklahoma? Huh! My old boyfriend is selling insurance while his nitwit wife and three kids makes his life even more miserable. Naw. They think I'm a star and going back home would only mean I failed. When you come to Hollywood, you come to become a star. Haven't you heard? You can never go back home."

Clara pulled a chair close to the Formica-topped table and sat down, looking Joyce directly in her eyes.

"Joyce, I'm going to make it. I know I am!"

"I honestly believe you ain't shittin'," she gulped down the cold beer. "You've got a lot of class and everything else it takes. You'd better not put down being black, either. Around here it's best to play up everything you got!"

Clara started to snap at her, but realized Joyce was only trying to help. So what if she did have talent. She was black and beautiful and that's what big time producers would see first. So, why not take advantage of it.

"C'mon, let's get ready. I know an outdoor cafe on Sunset that should be a good start. Yours is the first room on the left," she said as she reached over and kissed Clara on the cheek, "so go get yourself lookin' sexy!"

That was the second time Joyce had affectionately touched her! All Clara needed was to be shackin' with a lesbian—a gray one at that! She would have to be cautious but maybe there wasn't anything to it. White folks kiss anyone and everyone, she said to herself as she thought about the white people she had known in college.

There were too many other things on her mind to worry about Joyce.

7...

It was seven-thirty p.m. when the girls stepped out of the apartment. The air was quite cool and a slight breeze made it even cooler. Clara covered her backless white halter-topped Ciana jump suit with a white beaded sweater. The wind caught her dark curls that flopped in the air but every strain was in place when they got in Joyce's 1967 blue Ford

Mustang.

"Since I live so close to work, I decided a long time ago to leave the car at home and walk. It saves me money. Besides, it's about the only exercise I get."

Joyce was dressed in a lightweight black pajama style pant suit that didn't do much for her. But Clara had come to the conclusion that Joyce was just a small town girl and the glitter and glamour of Hollywood couldn't change her. She looked like Maude's daughter on the television show. Nothing special, until she fixed herself up.

Before long they were sitting at the Melting Pot an outdoor cafe on LaCienega, trying not to look like two starlets.

"Paul Newman comes here every now and then. Once I was sitting over near where that black couple is sitting and he brushed by in a safari jacket and cut off jeans! Can you dig that! Paul Newman!" she exclaimed.

"I'd rather see Fred Williamson in one of those short brown leather jackets and tight brown leather pants with one of those long thin cigars hangin' out the side of his mouth any day!" returned Clara.

"Well," Joyce agreed, "I wouldn't mind that myself!"

They laughed and joked as they sat sipping Blue Nun wine.

The traffic was picking up as the Bentleys, Mercedes and Rolls Royces began to increase in number.

"Who can afford all those big cars, Joyce?"

"You can believe that many of these people drivin' 'em can't! This is one town where everyone 'goes Hollywood' whether they can afford it or not. Everyone trips out over something. You wait until you're here a while. The tinsel bug will hit you square in your ass like it hits everyone else. It's the phoniest place in the world. Most people are miserable but they're so strung out on every pill, powder or weed that they can't tell the real from the make-believe."

"That's how whitey lives," Clara remarked sarcastically.

"Hold on, Clara. Blacks are just as phony out here as whites. Phoniness doesn't discriminate. You can't believe them either! Why they'd just as soon cut your neck as anyone else and call you 'Soul Sister' all along. Just a town full of freaks!"

"Now, now, Joyce," said a slim blond man who leaned over to whisper in her ear.

"Hi, Mr. Milner," said Joyce warmly.

Carl Milner had the classic white businessman look. His tailored tweed suit was cut to a "T" and a diamond tictac kept his gray striped tie neatly against a white shirt. At one time, he was Hollywood's top producer. But a few failures dropped him into the ranks of has beens. His eyes bulged as he stared at Clara. It was obvious that he was waiting for an introduction.

"Carl Milner meet Clara Brown. She's new in town, an aspiring actress," Joyce boasted.

"Just what I'm looking for in my new movie," Milner said as he pulled a red director's chair from a near-by table and sat close to Clara.

"Oh, really," Clara answered eagerly as she crossed her legs and sat back in the chair.

Milner's eyes were glued to her slim figure. Clara felt uneasy as she followed his eyes cross her breasts and fall on her slim thighs. She sat forward with her hands under her chin.

"What did you have in mind?" she asked.

"Do you think you could handle a leading role?"

"I know I can!" Clara answered excitedly.

Joyce didn't look as excited as Clara.

"Don't come on too strong, Carl," Joyce warned.

"Why, Joyce, you know me better than that," he reassured her.

"That's right. I *know* you!"

"Don't listen to her, Clara. You're a lovely woman and I can give you the start you need. It's hard to get a break around here. Why don't we go to my apartment and you can look over the script.

Clara was excited as she looked at Joyce.

"Well, what have I got to lose!" she said as she shrugged her shoulders.

"Go right ahead," answered Joyce cautiously as if giving consent to a daughter who is going out on a date she doesn't really approve of.

"Just don't loose your key!" she warned.

"Joyce, I'll take good care of her," Carl smiled quickly.

Joyce didn't bother to answer as Carl held Clara's arm and led her to his steel gray Mercedes.

Quiet fell over the city as Joyce slept between her red silk sheets. She heard Clara's soft footsteps as she walked up the stairs. The digital clock next to Joyce's bed read one forty-five. Even though Joyce wanted to ask Clara what happened she also knew that it would be time to get up before long and that sleep was more important.

Five hours later, the clock buzzed loudly. Joyce was still sleepy when she slowly turned off the alarm.

She looked around at her drab furniture. Her black suit had fallen on the floor at the foot of her bed. Her night out was no big thing but maybe Clara had something worth telling. Joyce knew what to expect from Carl but Clara didn't. Somehow Joyce couldn't bring herself to disappointing Clara. A cotton housecoat lay on the bed and Joyce wrapped it around her naked white body as she waddled into Clara's room.

"Clara, wake up, Black Beauty. The coach has turned into a pumpkin and it's time to go back to the presser."

"M-m-m," moaned Clara sleepily.

"Wake up, Clara," urged Joyce as she climbed into bed with Clara. She lay next to Clara shaking her gently.

Clara's eyes opened slowly to find a white chick laying next to her.

Clara sat up in her sheer pink negligee. She didn't want to look too upset but she tried to be cool.

"Already?" she moaned.

"Yes. Sam the slave driver is waiting!" Joyce laughed.

"Last night was great! For once I've met a man who treated me like a woman!"

"And you read for a part?"

"Oh, yes. It's a great part. A young girl jilted by her lover who wants to commit suicide."

"Oh how dull," answered Joyce. "I hate to tell you this but Carl has been carrying the script around for years. I auditioned for the same part six months ago."

"You did?"

"Yeah. He's a nice guy but he's going no place. Clara, you can't believe people out here. C'mon, the slobs are waiting!"

"Shit!" said Clara as she threw her white fluffy pillow on the floor.

Sam was waiting for Joyce and Clara as they rushed into the cleaners.

"Five minutes late already!" he bellowed as he pointed to the large clock on the wall.

"I know, I know, Sam! But we're here!" Joyce said as she pinched his cheek.

Clara didn't have time to butter up an old white man so she walked past him and began sorting clothes.

Every chance she had was spent at the pay phone. She had brought a portfolio of her best pictures with her from Gary and had sent pictures and resumes to every agent in town. For two weeks she called every theatrical agent hoping for some sign of encouragement.

By the third week, she was ready to give up.

"I can't take it any more, Joyce!" she said suddenly as she burst out in tears as the steam flew out of the presser.

"I'm sick of this damn job. No one will even call or let me know that they've looked at my pictures," she sobbed. "Weren't you the one who said black was 'in'? It's in alright—in a cleaners! Fuck it, just fuck it!"

"Hold on, honey. Hold on! Don't let it get to you! That's what happened to us failures," said Joyce as she held Clara by the shoulders. "Just be cool. Things gotta break soon."

"But when?" sobbed Clara, "when?"

"What's this!" stormed Sam as he stood behind Joyce and Clara. "Can't you cry on your own time? Why on mine? The machines, ladies, the machines! *P-ss-ss-t! P-ss-ss-t!* The lovely sound of the machines pressing, pressing. Making money, ladies, making money!"

"Sam, can't you see she's upset!"

"Upset?" questioned Sam.

"Yeah, it's that time of the month."

"Oh," said Sam sympathetically. "What am I gonna do with you two? Why didn't I hire all men, already? he asked as he snapped his suspenders and walked away, shaking his head.

"Pull out of it, Clara. Only the movies makes Hollywood look glamorous."

Sam's voice could hardly be heard above the other pressing machines.

"Clara!" he yelled. "Clara!"

"Huh?" she cried as she wiped her tears with her sweaty denim blouse.

"Telephone. And make it quick," he ordered.

"TELEPHONE?" both girls spoke at the same

time.

"Quick! Wipe that running nose and dry those eyes," smiled Joyce.

"You think this is it?" Clara asked tearfully.

"Hell, I don't know until you answer the damn phone!"

Clara rushed to the phone still wiping her face as she held the receiver.

"Hell-o-o," she stuttered. "Yes, yes. This is she. What? You mean it? Yes. Yes. I'll be there. No. No, I won't be late," she smiled as she slammed the receiver down.

Sam trucked behind her as she ran to tell Joyce the good news.

"Joyce!" she screamed. "I got a job! I got a job!"

"No shit!" Joyce yelled as she threw her arms around her. Sam stood in bewilderment as he scratched his head.

"A Mr. Brisco wants me to come right down to his office on West Sunset right now!"

"Oh, great! I told you to hold on!"

"I've got to go home and change!" Clara realized as she looked at her wrinkled jeans.

"What about the pants, Miss Brown?"

"The pants? Sam, this is what I think of the pants! Clara threw a rumpled pair of pants on the machine and pulled the lid down. Steam flew everywhere causing Sam to cough as he rushed to release the top before the pants burned.

"Screw a pair of pants!" Clara yelled as she rushed out the door.

8...

Clara was right on time as she walked off the elevator at the second floor. A tall, light brown-skinned black man weighing about two hundred fifty pounds was coming out of an office. They smiled at each other as Clara spoke.

"Are you Mr. Brisco?"

"No. I'm Ben Calder. Brisco is next door," he said as every strain of his brown bush sparkled as if he had just sprayed it with Afro-Sheen. "Are you an actress?"

"No," she smiled, "But I hope to become one soon. I think I've got a job."

"A sister as foxy as you shouldn't have any problems."

76

"Well, I've had enough so far to last a lifetime. But wish me luck!"

"You got that!" Ben smiled, as he walked away.

Clara straightened her white Swiss polka dot dress and pushed her purse under her arm before knocking on the door. A few seconds later a mild male's voice called for her to enter.

Once inside, she was greeted by a handsome white man who appeared to be in his forties. He wasn't a flashy dresser but Clara could tell by his dark blue suit that he had good taste. His brown hair was cut neatly and not too long.

Brisco stood about an inch shorter than Clara, but smiled warmly when she entered as he rose from his desk and extended his hand to greet her.

Clara nervously shook his hand and sat on the chair next to his huge mahogany desk. His office was plush with leather furnishings and a deep brown shag rug. The opaque curtains were open, exposing Hollywood's smog filled sky as the sun peeped through the clouds.

Brisco's smile made Clara uneasy. Again she had to stand the stares of a white man. And she felt as if he were undressing her as he looked her up and down.

"Miss Brown, your resume looks good and your pictures look even better. You've had a lot of experience," he said with encouragement.

"Yes, I have, and I'm anxious to get a part. Anything would do. I know I have to start at the bottom, but I'm a hard worker," she said with wide open eyes.

"Well, it may not be as hard or as long as it has been. Let me make a call."

Clara sat nervously as Brisco talked to a producer. She listened as he praised the fine black woman sitting in his office. Within minutes, the deal was made and Clara waited excitedly for him to tell her about her part.

Brisco smiled broadly. "Paul always thinks I'm sending him someone with no talent. But, you heard me reassure him, didn't you?"

Clara nodded with a smile.

"Take a look at these contracts," said Brisco as he shoved a pen and three copies of the contract toward her.

Clara's eagerness showed as she quickly skimmed the papers.

"Wait, let's give you a name that suits you. Why not Carla? Yes. Carla Brown. Is that alright with you?"

"Well, I guess so. Yes, I like the way that sounds," she answered as she signed her new name. "I guess it won't take me long to get used to it."

Brisco watched Carla sign the paper, then walked toward her chair and stood in back of her.

"Now, it's time for you to pay me, Miss Brown," he said with a sly look in his eyes.

"Do what?" Clara asked with a puzzled look on her face.

"Pay me. You see," he said as he moved his slender fingers along her shoulders, "I own ten per cent of you and I just got you a job. But I haven't been paid.

"The first rule to learn out here is that an agent will work like hell for you if he's paid well. And a sexy looking black woman like you, desperately trying to make it to the top, can make it fast if she pays well. Know what I'm drivin' at, Carla?"

Carla froze in her chair as her body stiffened from head to foot.

"Relax, Carla, we're going to have a long, long life together," he whispered as he kissed her neck. Once again, that white man's smell filled her nostrils. She wanted to vomit as his scent overpowered her but her career meant more than losing her breakfast!

"Aren't we, Carla?" he insisted.

"Yes," she whispered. "Just tell me what you want."

"Why don't you just unzip this feminine little dress and I think the rest will follow. Now relax, honey, and remember. I'm going to make you a star."

Clara rose slowly and nervously unzipped her dress. She didn't wear a bra but wiggled out of her black bikini panties. Was it worth it, she thought as tears destroyed her makeup. Her dress fell to the floor wrapped around her slim ankles.

Brisco's clammy hands slid around her sides and squeezed her breasts. She was ashamed to look down and see a white man's hands covering her pretty brown skin. Her nipples pointed, infuriating her even more as his forefingers rubbed them over and over.

"Your body is beautiful, Carla," he panted as excitement turned his face red with heat. "Just lay down on this couch and give me what I want!"

Leather had never been colder or stickier to Carla. She could imagine what laying on a steel slab would be like. If she resisted him, she knew he might throw her out. If she got hot, he might like it too much. She figured this was one time playing it safe was her best bet. Maybe he wouldn't screw her again. Maybe . . .

It only took Brisco a few seconds to strip before he pounced on top of her.

He continued to drive his sharp teeth in her ear as his hands played with her skin like a child playing with clay.

Bastard! she wanted to yell. *Motherfuckin' bastard!* For centuries black women had to screw their masters against their will. She was not different from the slave women of plantations or maids in rich white folks' kitchens. *Bastard! Motherfuckin' bastard!*

"Relax, baby," he slobbered as he grew hard. He was ready now, and as she relaxed she felt herself coming. It wouldn't be as rough as he thought. Now he could slide right in her and drown!

"Over! It's over!" Clara whispered, fighting back tears. Her nails had long since stopped digging into his flesh. "Do I get the part?" she sneered with clenched teeth.

Brisco was still freaked out over screwing this beautiful black woman.

"Well, do I get the part, Mr. Brisco?"

"What do you think?" he said as he kissed her mascara stained cheek.

As Carla closed the door to Brisco's office, she held her head down in shame. Her back was turned to Ben as he got off the elevator and walked toward her.

"Hey, you look mighty sad. Sorry you didn't get the part," he said sympathetically.

"Cut the sorry crap! I got the part!" she mumbled angrily.

"Oh. I get it." Ben paused when he realized what had happened. He took her by the shoulders but she never raised her eyes. She was too embarrassed to let a brother know what she had done.

"Hey, sweet sister," he said as he held her chin up to look into her eyes. "We all got to pay some dues to get where we want. Look. Let me buy you a drink and . . ."

"What the hell do *you* want from me?"

"Wow! You don't have to act like a nigger with me. You look like you need a friend. That's all."

"I'm sorry. I guess I'm just pissed off with men messin' over me," she paused. "You know what I really want to say, don't you?"

They both smiled as she pushed her pocketbook under her arm.

"C'mon. You need a drink and a friend all at the same time."

Ben's 1975 burgundy Riviera cruised through the busy traffic as the late afternoon sun slipped into the blue clouds. Clara felt better as she sank into the soft red bucket seat. What a difference from the cold black leather couch. Within a short time they were stopping in the parking lot of a cozy club off LaCienega.

Once inside, a blonde hostess in a tight white knitted dress showed them to a table near a stained glass window. Ben ordered for the both of them, then lit up a cigarette. Carla didn't smoke but sat twisting the ashtray on the small black table.

"Okay, Clara . . ."

"It's Carla now," she interrupted.

"Man, he changed that, too!" he answered.

"Right now I don't know who I am."

"What did I tell you. We all have to kiss an ass or two to get where we want to go."

"Look, Ben. Don't hand me that crap. I've read movie magazines, *The Inquirer, Sepia, Players, Jet, Ebony, Black Stars* and all the rest and I haven't heard or read about any black female stars going through what I have!" she insisted.

"Baby, you can't believe that mess. Only a fly on the wall can tell you what they went through. Do you think when they're on top makin' twenty grand a picture or more that they're gonna talk about the bullshit they went through to get there? Shit no! I'm not sayin' they had it as rough as you but they went through hell if doin' nothin' but takin' bullshit roles. And, Carla, you ain't seen nothin' yet!"

"I don't want to lose Clara Brown, Ben. I don't want to lose the real me. Besides, how worse can it get?"

"Carla, when I started out I didn't have my own business. I was in the back, the back of the office with the worst clients. But they kept me 'cause I was their token nigger. Their show piece. But in time I showed them that the filth was theirs, not

83

mine, and I winded up with my own business, telling rich white folks how to spend their dough.''

"Clara smiled for the first time in hours. "I guess every business has rotten apples," she confessed.

"Damn straight!'' he agreed as he pounded his fist on the table. "Just don't forget who you are and where you're going. And when you get to the top, *you* call the shots!''

"But, you gotta fight to stay there. And black folks got to fight twice as hard," she said as the waitress brought their drinks.

"Well, baby, life's a fight and if it's worth enough to ya', you'll get out there and punch the hell out of it. Now, let's drink to the star.''

"Thanks, Ben. You're the friend I need," she smiled.

... 9

For the next three weeks Carla was busy. She had to go through hell with Brisco. Just to get a one line walk-on meant screwing him on the cold leather couch. And the weight of his medium frame got heavier each time. She felt like she was being caught in a vise just waiting for the pressure to be released.

This is the last time, she thought. He can't make me go through this every time. He just can't!

But, she had another think coming! It got to the point that when Ben called she pleaded with Joyce to tell him that she was not home or sleeping. How could she tell the only together black man that she had met about being less than a woman—a black woman? She was ashamed to talk to him and she knew she couldn't talk to Joyce.

It didn't take long for the hatred to build up in her like a volcano ready to explode. Any day the lid would blow off and the hot lava of frustration would fly in every direction. She had started smoking and had begun drinking more.

Ben was no fool and Joyce had run out of excuses when he called.

The phone rang one hazy Saturday morning. Early September in Los Angeles still meant warm days and cool nights.

R-r-ring! R-r-ring! rattled the phone, waking only Joyce.

"Shit! Who in the hell is that?" she said, more pissed off than sleepy.

"Hello," she answered quickly.

"My, you sound wide awake at eight thirty," Ben said in a dry tone.

"Oh, Ben. Well ah—it really isn't pleasant enough around here to sleep. To tell you the truth, she worries the hell out of me."

"Why not stop covering for her? You know you ain't her mama!"

"No. I'm almost her color, but not her mother. You've got that right, Mr. Calder!" she answered

86

sharply.

"Look, we both care about Carla, so let's be honest with each other!"

Joyce paused. "You're right, Ben. I'm sorry. But I was only following her instructions. She wants that big break so badly but she knows that the real Ms. Brown is harder to find once Brisco finishes with her. She doesn't know what to do!"

"Yeah. I got that feeling too," he said with concern.

"Can't you do something?" she pleaded.

"Nothing short of castrating Brisco would do!" he threatened.

"That's for damn sure!" she agreed.

"Joyce, wake Carla and tell her to go shopping or something. Say you're going to St. Mary's Garden or Decorator's Row. Any place she might be interested in. Make sure she's ready at eleven o'clock. I'll be over just before you go. Now, don't mess me up. Something's got to be done. I'm afraid of what she might do."

Ben wasn't much for "CP time." If he said he'd be there a few minutes before eleven o'clock, he meant it.

Carla jumped with surprise when she answered the door bell. "Ben!" she exclaimed.

He looked more like a husky football player in tan slacks and a tan print kiana shirt that was

opened, showing off his bronze muscular chest.
She could go for him but all she dared to think of
was her career. Scully had messed up her mind one
time and no repeat performance was needed now.

"C'mon, get your bag. You're coming with me,"
he ordered. "And don't start acting like a nigger!"

What else could she do, she thought. He was too
big to fight.

Before long they were out of the city and travelling through the smog of the San Diego Freeway.
They whizzed past the sprinklers that drenched the
freeways' greenery to prevent fires due to lack of
rain in weeks. The sun was getting hotter, but as
they neared the ocean the cool air sailed through
the car relieving their pent-up emotions.

The radio had blasted rock music for more than
an hour, giving both of them an excuse not to talk.
But now that they weren't up-tight it was time to
break the silence.

"Where are we going?" Clara asked as she turned
toward Ben.

"To the Rusty Pelican in Laguna Beach," he
said, glancing at her orange midriff top that could
barely hold the fullness of her breasts.

Carla knew as much as she did before and decided to change the radio station to something
softer.

Within the next hour they were passing oil rig-

By Bobbye B. Vance

gers and surfers. One was as plentiful as the others.

There was one thing Clara was checking out. Black folks didn't seem to go in for riding waves as much as whites. Even the last minute vacationers they passed were white.

"Is this one of your out of the way places you take your white female clients?" she muttered.

Ben really didn't think she deserved an answer but it was time to get her on the right course.

"Are you white?"

"I've got enough white in me. And even more since Brisco became my agent!" she said as her voice trailed away.

"Well, there ain't too many of us around nowadays that don't have a few drops," he slapped back at her. "And I don't take any one here. I usually come here alone. It's too mellow a place to waste it on somebody who might not appreciate it."

Ben's Riviera slowed down as his eyes caught the words, RUSTY PELICAN. He turned cautiously into the parking lot and parked facing the dock.

A row of cabin cruisers and sail boats bobbed up and down in the water as the sun's reflection glistened like aluminum foil floating in the gray-blue water. The whole area looked like a scene from "Jaws" as the boat owners in jeans, windbreakers, and tennis shoes joked on the docks about their sailing ventures and fishing jaunts.

89

"You know, only honkies can stand around this time of day and talk about adventures on the high seas. What a life!" she said with envy.

"I can dig it!" Ben smiled, "But you're out here just like them so they ain't got nothin' on you, Ms. Brown!"

"You may be right, but I don't own nothin' rockin' back and forth in that water," she answered quickly.

"You don't know what *they* own. Besides, give yourself time. Who knows? You might own a yacht in a year's time!" he said with a wide grin.

"If I own that ten per cent of me that Brisco owns now, I'd be happy," she said in a dry voice.

Ben didn't answer. Instead, he got out his flashy Riviera and walked around to open her door. She held his hand as if holding on for security and never let go until inside the rustic restaurant.

Once inside, a white hostess in a short orange tight suit showed them up the dark, wide wooden-slat staircase and into a cozy lounge with a rock fireplace and picture window view of the harbor lined with boats longing to be splashing through the Pacific's waters.

They sat at a small table placed against the window.

"This place really makes you feel kinda like you're away from it all. Look at the beams in the ceiling and everything looks sorta slow and easy," Carla said.

"Yeah, look at those sail boats. Just gliding along," Ben said softly. "Free and easy. But that's what the ocean does to you. Makes you feel so high. No cares, no worries."

Carla paused. "Right now my high comes in a different form."

"That's what I want to talk to you about," Ben said in a businesslike tone.

The waitress interrupted them and a few minutes later brought two drinks. Ben gave in and handed Carla a cigarette. She puffed more than she inhaled but she was looking sexy if nothin' else.

They drank and talked for two hours as crafts large and small passed for their inspection.

"You and Joyce really tricked me this time!" she said as she shook her head and twisted her mouth.

"What else could we do?" he asked with hunched shoulders. "Besides, Joyce is worried, too. You've got to admit that she didn't have to take you in. She did it because she knew you were new in town, set on being a star and without a dime. She's been down that same road . . ."

"And been messed over too," she interrupted.

"So, you can't blame her for caring. Can you?"

Carla shook her head 'no' while watching a white

motor boat whiz past a sailboat causing it to rock from side to side.

"Even the heavy drinking and smoking has her worried."

"Well, she worries me, too!" she quipped.

"What do you mean by that?" Ben sat back comfortably in his orange director's chair with a concerned look on his face. "She seems O.K. to me."

"Well, it may be my imagination but she kisses a little too much," she said out the corner of her mouth.

"Who?" he asked with interest.

"Me!" Carla pounded her fingers against her chest.

"You're jiving," he smiled.

"It's not funny." She didn't think he'd believe her. "Well, it doesn't happen often and she doesn't kiss me on the lips or anything."

Ben's roar turned every white head in the place! Carla was embarrassed and leaned over, patting his strong hands.

"Will you shut up before we get put out!" she insisted. "Sh-h-h, Ben, please!"

His roar died to a mellow laugh.

"Now, this isn't funny, well, maybe it's no big thing. But, she just feels a need to touch my arm or softly kiss my cheek when she's excited or I'm sad.

And it's buggin' the hell out of me. As I said, it doesn't happen that often," she paused. "But I sleep kinda light!" she added with a deep Southern accent.

"Don't worry. White folks are like that. You kiss a nigger like that and they'll be all up side your head."

"Well, I wouldn't say that. But, there's a right time for everything. Maybe I'm just over sensitive."

"Could be," he agreed.

"But every part she's had in the movies, she's played a lesbian."

Ben looked at her seriously. Carla had enough problems with men and he didn't want her to get uptight over nothing. He sat forward and looked dead in her eyes.

"Carla, this isn't Gary, Indiana. Now, before you get uppity with me you better get one thing straight. This is California. People come out here for ten million and one reasons. You don't question anyone's life style. You don't have a right to. There're blacks who'd say you're crazy for trying to do what you're doin' *and* the way you're doin' it. So, don't prejudge Joyce or anyone else. Baby, if she was hot for you, you can be damn sure she wouldn't be lettin' me butt in. You just better look around before you go off the deep end! Getting to the top isn't worth losing yourself or anyone close to you." He paused to light another cigarette, but puffed away while he finished his sentence. "My Grandmother Carrie used to say, 'the friends you make goin' up are the same ones you gonna meet comin' down and you betta belie-e-ve dat!' "

Carla was silent as she crossed her legs and slumped in her chair. Ben didn't need to say another word. His strength even when talking was too much for her. If she had an ounce of his strength, she'd be hell!

"You getting tired or are you feeling better?" Ben asked.

"Feelin' better," Carla admitted. "But there is one thing I need to keep me goin', Ben."

"What is it, lady?" he smiled.

"For you to help me against Brisco."

"Baby, you know that honky rubs me the wrong way!" His jaws were tight!

"I'd deal with him myself, but . . ."

"But you're a woman, not Muhammad Ali. A black woman fights enough battles. That's what I'm here for, Carla. Just lean on me baby, I'll fight your battles. Dealing with Brisco will be a pleasure. What he needs is his balls cut off!" he said with contempt.

"Then, will you be my manager? I can make it with you takin' care of me. I need you, Ben!"

Her words rang in his ear as the liquor filled his

head. They had been together enough times but Ben had never tried to get closer than a kiss. He couldn't help but want to make love to her. He'd come on so strong as a friend when they met that he was fighting the friend image. The last time he was a chick's friend was when he was in high school. In those days being a friend was what the dudes would tell the girls. Once they believed the friend line, they'd be screwin' in hallways or in the back seats of cars. He wanted Carla and she'd had enough liquor to want him right in the middle of the Rusty Pelican!

But as she thought of it, she wondered if he'd think about her and Brisco. Ben moved to the chair next to her and held her chin in his large hand. Carla knew what was next and she didn't resist his wet tongue as it slowly slipped between her lips and touched her tongue. She tried to swallow it as he held her close. Now, even if a few honkies in the lounge stared at them, they didn't give a damn. For a few minutes nothing else mattered except the vibrations of need that flowed between them.

10...

Monday morning was brighter for Carla. She could tell Brisco to kiss *her* ass now, but she still had to be cool. After the weekend with Ben she was looking at herself again. The real Ms. Brown. She *was* black and beautiful and talented.

She had an appointment with a Mr. Lewis, a producer, at ten o'clock sharp near the Screen

By Bobbye B. Vance

Actor's Guild.

Every strain of her hair was piled in curls on top
of her head and her canary yellow dress hugged her
ass tightly.

"Mr. Lewis?" she asked hesitantly as she peeked
in the open door marked room twenty.

"Come in, my child," said the thin, balded eccentric. He rose politely, showing his shortness.
His glasses sat on the tip of his nose and he looked
over them as he admired Carla's honey brown
smooth skin.

The office was eccentric as Lewis. A silver tea
set covered a table on the left while antique office
furniture and pictures of mountain scenes added to
the dullness.

"Can I get you some tea, Miss Brown?" he asked
in a high voice.

"No, thank you, Mr. Lewis," she smiled. A good
stiff drink would have been more like it!

"I'd really like to hear about the part . . ."

"Oh, oh yes. Well, first, why don't you sit here
in front of my desk."

He walked toward her and placed his arm on
the wing-backed chair.

"Thank you," said Carla, watching him walk
nervously back to his soft leather chair.

"Perhaps you're interested in why I contacted
Mr. Brisco."

97

Carla nodded.

"Well, my dear. I've seen many parts you've played and well, you ah, have a delicacy that intrigues me. I, ah, can't put it in words but your sweet human qualities are precisely what I've looked all over for. My picture needs that touch. It needs your warm qualities to bring the audience to its feet with applause and raves."

Carla was digging every word and grinned with pleasure as Lewis showered her with praise.

"I wish my father was here, Miss Brown. He taught me all I know," he said as he pointed to the picture behind his desk. "He'd be impressed by your talents," he continued. "He knew an artist when he saw one!"

"Why, thank you," she beamed. No modesty this time.

"I, er, would like for you to read a few lines from my movie to, er, let you feel the part I'd like for you to portray."

"Oh, that's why I'm here, Mr. Lewis," she said with enthusiasm as she placed her purse and portfolio on the corner of the glass covered desk.

Such a gentleman, Clara thought as she felt herself acting too much like a young girl. Mr. Lewis saw her as a sophisticated woman. A lady, she thought to herself. So, she'd better play it to death.

"Tell me about the part, sir," she said as if from Boston's most proper finishing schools.

He handed her a script and told her to look over the lines he had marked. She shook her head as if finding no problems with it.

"My dear child. Perhaps before we go any further I might explain one thing."

Carla's ears perked up, waiting to hear Lewis' words.

He continued with his proper self.

"My leading lady does, ah," he fluttered with embarrassment, "ah," he continued, "well, disrobe."

Carla's smile hadn't worn off yet. She felt that Lewis' shyness made it tough for him to do or say anything that might offend her.

"Oh, that doesn't bother me," she reassured him.

"Thank God," he sighed in relief. "Then, you wouldn't mind . . ." he couldn't get the words out.

"Not at all, Mr. Lewis," she reassured him. Carla wanted this part! And she told herself the tea sopper in front of her didn't mean any harm.

"Nudity for nudity's sake is repulsive and certainly not artistic, Mr. Lewis. But, if it's to make the character look believable and doesn't lower my standards then I see nothing wrong with it."

"I'm so glad you feel that way." He tried to

hold back his smile. "The other thing that concerns me terribly is the fact that so many young ladies have walked through that door looking extremely well developed. And later I found that all development was manufactured. Er, if you know what I mean?" he questioned with embarrassment.

"Padded," she said as if interpreting his statement.

"Precisely!" he said as he folded his hands slowly. "You, ah, wouldn't mind . . ."

"Taking my clothes off now?" she asked as she put the script on the table.

"Now, you needn't rush these things," he said as his eyes batted. "I just want to be sure!" He fumbled with his tie as if loosening it would have slowed down his pressure.

"Oh, I understand, quite well." Carla couldn't really see any harm as she reached behind her to unzip her dress, which wiggled its way down her slim figure and to the oriental rug beneath her. Lewis smiled broadly with pleasure, then motioned with one finger for her to remove her scanty white bra. There she stood, naked again! But so psyched out that it didn't phase her in the least. Lewis' eyes danced with excitement. He wanted her to move closer to drink in as much of her full breasts as he could.

"Lovely, my dear, lovely," he admired as his

pale white skin began to take on a pinkish color. "Just read what I have marked off, the part about the girl trying to convince her lover that he needn't be shy about making love to her." He leaned back in his chair. This was getting too good for him and at this moment he didn't want to miss a trick. "Go right ahead, my dear."

Clara's bra had settled on her hips above her nylon panties. She pushed it up and clutched it under her breasts, causing them to look even larger. She awkwardly held the script in her other hand. She was so into getting the part that she didn't notice the old man getting redder than a beet. That always gives white folks away. A candidate for the cemetery, but still trying to get his kicks the only way he could.

Lewis wanted to climb over his mahogany desk and dive on Carla as his heart pounded away at his rib cage. Beads of sweat were forming at his temples and if his bifocals could have fogged up, they would have. Carla read on and on with emotion that could have upset a corpse.

" 'Easy, baby. Everything's gonna be okay. Just relax. Oh, yes,' " she purred like a kitten. " 'Just relax. Touch me, baby, yes, feel me, feel me. O-o-o-ow, baby'." Her body swayed like the gentle palm tree on a soft windy day. Her eyes were closed with every moan as her words trailed away.

101

The sudden sound of a gasp broke her trend of thought. Lewis was about to piss in his pants! His glass fell to the desk pad below when Carla moaned. He was drunk with passion.

Carla couldn't believe her eyes! Lewis sat shaking as if he'd just climaxed.

"Ah!" gasped Carla in disgust. She was breathing so fast that her words were getting in her way.

"You! You! You geriatric freak! I should have known what was on your cobwebbed mind!" She threw the script at him, missing him by inches. If he hadn't been shaking it would have landed square on his bald head. Carla didn't think she could dress so fast but the adrenalin had built up to the point where she could have whizzed through anything!

"Who in the hell do you think you are?" she asked as she scrambled for her purse and portfolio. "Why, you motherfucker . . ." She was too enraged to speak further. It wouldn't have done any good anyway because Lewis was so spastic and out of it that he wouldn't have heard a word!

The door slammed with fury as Carla seethed with anger.

Rain was falling lightly as Carla stomped out of the cab and marched up the white cement stairs to Joyce's apartment. She didn't see or feel a drop. The only thing on her mind was being screwed over again. How much more could she take, she asked herself as she rammed the key into the keyhole.

The stillness of the house was broken by her portfolio which she flung in the corner. She took two steps at a time as she raced up the stairs. Joyce had stayed home from work that day and the sound of Carla's entrance forced her from the kitchen.

"What's got over you?" she yelled, looking all wide-eyed up through the wrought iron staircase railing. Clara moved with the swiftness of a panther.

"I said, what's up?"

The volcano finally erupted and Joyce soon found that she had better get out of the way! By the time she reached Carla's room, clothes were flying.

"I can't hassle this shit!" Carla screamed as she threw her clothes in her red suitcase. "Nobody thinks I'm an actress but me. All these white bastards want to do is paw all over me or watch me strip!" She stopped and shoved her hands on her hips. "Girl, you don't know what I went through today!"

She was pissed off alright, as anger seethed out of every pore in her body. She re-enacted for Joyce the degrading scene with Lewis, which made her more upset. Joyce shook her head as she leaned against the bedroom door with all ears perked.

"Carla," she said, "I told you it wasn't easy out here."

Carla rummaged through her small closet. Joyce's words sailed over her head. They weren't about to calm her down.

"Not easy! It's damn near impossible! Everybody's trying to hassle me!" Her energy was slipping but she kept moving.

"Ben's handin' me the 'keep on pushin'' line. You handin' me the keep on pushin' line. Well, I'm tired of pushin'. And if you really wanna know. I'm gettin' more pushed than anyone else and I'm pretty damn tired!"

Wrinkles covered her smooth honey forehead as her lips tightened.

Joyce slid to the floor and sat with her hands running through her hair.

"Why don't you call Ben?" Joyce demanded.

"Oh, he's out of town today. Besides, his opinion is just a chocolate-covered version of yours, anyway," she said sarcastically.

Joyce had learned a long time ago that it was cooler to let her rant and rave because sooner or later she would run out of steam. As Carla quieted down, she slumped in a soft cushioned chair between the dresser and the red curtains that covered the windows.

"What's the use!" she cried as she threw her

hands in the air. "What the hell is the use in goin' through this. I'm goin' back to Gary. At least I was somebody there."

"And to Scully, I bet."

"Yes," she said sadly. "And to Scully. There are too many black men in prison now who need somebody to care about them. And he's one of them. I guess trying to help myself just isn't the answer." She sat forward with her hands covering her eyes. They were moist with tears when Joyce slowly rose and walked over to cradle her in her arms.

"Just hold on, honey," she insisted as she gently squeezed Carla's shoulders.

"I can't, I can't," she wept. "They're takin' everything out of me. It's too damn hard to hold on when everyone is pulling you away from what you want. Nobody wants anybody to get ahead. Everyone *wants* you to fail like they did. Oh, and don't think white folks have a monopoly on that! Huh, shit no!" She gently broke Joyce's hold and leaned back in the chair wiping her eyes. Joyce sat on the bed and looked at her with a puzzled look on her face while Carla continued.

"Do you remember the day Ben took me to Paramount?"

Joyce nodded yes.

"Well, after that he dropped me off at a black

photographers'. Someone I'd bumped into coming out of Brisco's building one day. Well, he insisted that I needed some better pictures than the one I had and gave me his card. So, as I said, Ben dropped me off and I posed and posed. Renting those clothes took up most of my money I'd made from a couple of commercials. The fellow seemed harmless, kinda slim build with smooth brown skin, nice neat 'fro and all. Well, everything was goin' well in this little studio. But, I was so tired after three hours. He didn't have a bathroom or anything so I had been changing in front of him. Most photogs never hassled me, so I really wasn't worried. Besides, I was tired. Well, just as I was stepping out of this long sexy black dress he comes over to me and asks me if I'm lookin' for any action that would make me some good money. I said 'like what?' Now dig this," her eyes opened and she looked Joyce dead in her face. "Now listen. He said, 'I know a few gray dudes who lookin' for a mamma like you to make a few flicks. Just a coupla dudes you and I'll be right there snappin' away. There's more money in X-rated stuff than PG any day'." Joyce just shook her head. She wasn't too surprised but Carla was boiling again as she pounded her knees.

"Can you beat that! A brother, too!"

"Why didn't you say something before?" Joyce

asked.

" 'Cause that's when I was holdin' everything inside. And I'm not doin' that any more. Everyone else goes on about their business and I'm the one gettin' ulcers. Besides, I really wanted to block out the idea of someone black doin' me in, too. It's bad enough that I got whitey runnin' games on me. Now, I got to . . ."

A hurt look flashed across Joyce's face, making Carla realize that she was lumping all whites in one basket. She had to admit, with all her suspicions, Joyce had taken her in and helped her out. Maybe she was coming down too hard. But the damage was done and all she could do was say a few words.

"Look, Joyce. There are good and bad people in all colors. But, with the exception of you and Ben, and a sweet ole' black couple that picked me up in Vegas, I get kicked in the ass by dudes that don't do anything more than think of me as their whore."

Joyce had heard enough and slowly rose, walking toward the door and down the hall.

"Call Brisco," she said as if one last job would be the break.

"Don't even mention his name!" Carla yelled.

When Carla hit the front door with her bag in her hand, she was headed to the nearest bus stop.

She had made her decision to lleave Glittersville for the real sho' 'nuf like in Gary. At least, she knew who she was there. But as the door slammed behind her she gave the whole rotten idea second thoughts.

She threw down her suitcase and pocketbook in dejection.

"Oh, what's the use," she whimpered. "Joyce was right. You can't go home. You just can't go home." Tears flowed like the rain that was falling heavier. It was the first rain in weeks and Carla felt every drop now. Inside and out, the fight was gone. The lava stopped flowing.

She was discouraged but she had been discouraged before. Ben said everyone had to pay their dues, she thought. And she'd damn well paid enough!

She rummaged through her bag and found the key. By the time Joyce walked out of her room and peered over the balcony, Carla was dialing the phone.

She spoke slowly. "Brisco," she said between sobs. "Brisco, get me a job, quick! Forget all those bullshit jobs. Get me something good. No. I'll do whatever you want. Just get me something." Her voice was trembling as tears ran over the corners of her mouth. She had about as much strength as a wet rag and it was an effort to put the phone down. But, she did. Without even waiting for Brisco to say another word. All she knew was that it was time for Brisco to work for his ten per cent as much as she had to work.

II...

Carla was ready now! Ready to take a different look at the whole rotten industry. She was back at Brisco's office in a yellow two-piece suit with a flowered scarf around her neck.

"Why me?" she fumed. "Why, I put all my trust in you and you do this to me! If it's the last thing I do on the face of this earth, it's make you pay. So help me God, I'll make you pay!" The words of threats rolled off her tongue with the deadliness of a snake's venom.

"Great! Just Great!" clapped a tall, slim, white-headed producer in his gray flannel suit. He was one of Hollywood's top producers. Even though Brisco had a thing for black women he knew that

Carla had talent and that Les was strictly business. Being in one of his movies meant automatic stardom with an increase in percentage to boot! When Carla hit the top Brisco wouldn't settle for ten per cent.

Ben and Brisco stood at opposite ends of the plush office but clapped with approval at Carla's performance.

"Really, great for the first reading," Les said with surprise.

"You mean it?" Carla asked through a broad smile while she hugged the script. "Do I get the part then?"

"Wow! Not so fast," he warned with a smile. "You'll have to read again and then there's the matter of a screen test. But I feel confident that it will come off well. If you do as well on film as you did just now, you can consider yourself as having the part."

"Fantastic!" Ben shouted as he watched Carla give Les a gentle hug. She really bubbled with excitement when she turned toward Ben and gave him a kiss on his cheek. She didn't even look Brisco's way as he moved in between her and Ben and placed his arm around her shoulder in a fatherly manner. Her smile turned sour as he patted her shoulder gently.

"She's really hot now, Les. You've seen her

reviews. Nothin' but praise. Why, she's not going to come cheap but we can come to an agreement on that and . . ."

"Let's see the results of the screen test, first," Les interrupted.

"You'd better think about getting her under contract now. Say, a three picture deal?" Brisco suggested eagerly as greed filled his eyes.

Caution was written all over Les' face as he looked at Brisco. He felt that things would go well with Carla but nothing was sure except death and the landlord, so there was no need to sign a big contract. She had to prove herself to the public. Besides, all Brisco could see were dollar signs and he could care less than a damn about Carla. She was just his ticket to the top.

Ben smiled with approval as Les straightened out Brisco. Ben looked militant but his style was one of taking a back seat until his big chance was near. Carla wasn't used to his type. Her loud and rowdy niggers didn't get her any place so meeting Ben was really a change. His style was different but it seemed to work because he *was* where everyone wants to be—doing his own thing. Being her manager couldn't have come at a better time. Brisco would be getting greedy and she didn't want to have him pawing all over her! So if Ben could protect her everything would be cool.

112

"What would you like Carla to do?" Ben interrupted. Brisco didn't like his butting in. He looked at Ben with disgust and even when Les spoke he kept his eyes on Ben.

"Have her at the studio at nine sharp. Once we look at the tests, we'll get a better idea of how she comes off on the screen. And then we'll have a big party for the investors on Friday. I think they'd like to get a look at their star."

Carla was bursting with excitement. If she could have stood on the window ledge and shouted to the bustling city below, she would have! She was two steps from stardom and she was ready to let the whole world know about it.

They all agreed that she'd be at the studio and at the party.

"This calls for a celebration," smiled Ben as he shook Les' hand.

"I don't see why not," Les agreed, shaking Ben's hand firmly.

"Oh, wait, let me get my . . ." her words were cut off by her agent.

"Ah, Carla, I think *we* have some *business* first."

What in the hell is he talking about, thought Carla as she frowned.

"Business?" she asked, her eyes squinted.

"Oh, it won't take long," he answered casually. He looked at Ben with a smirk on his face.

113

"As Carla's manager, I think I have some say so over her so-called business affairs," Ben said as he walked toward Brisco with his arms folded across his broad chest.

"Oh, I don't deny that," answered Brisco. "But, I'm still her agent and there are some things just the two of us need to deal with." He was as sly as a fox and stood looking at the three of them as if he dared for anyone to cross him.

Carla stood trying to keep cool but she felt her body trembling. She didn't dare look at Ben or Les, but kept her eyes dead on the large picture window behind Brisco's desk. Why didn't Ben stand up to him, she asked herself. That was why she needed him. Was "white right" even for him? There must be a reason but she couldn't let on to Les that anything was wrong. The part meant too much for her.

Carla didn't see Brisco escort Ben and Les to the door. She didn't see the daggers coming out of Ben's eyes. He wanted to do him in right then and there. But the timing wasn't right. He couldn't blow Carla's big chance. Carla could only hear Brisco's words ringing in her ears until the slamming of the heavy door broke her concentration.

Brisco slowly walked behind her and gently squeezed her soft round buttocks. He wasn't surprised when she flinched because he knew that she couldn't stand his clammy white hands touching any part of her sexy brown body.

"Tch! Tch! Tch! Now, you didn't think that I would let you walk out of that door without my percentage worth? Did you?" He whispered in her ear sarcastically.

The sparkling starlet was burning. Just when she thought her problems were over with this honky she realized that she would never get away from his funcky touch. He'd pay, she told herself as she slowly unbuttoned the jacket of her suit. This cracker would pay!

Scully kept up with Carla's career while he was doing time. There wasn't too much he couldn't find out or get his hands on.

Being locked up was a trip for him but it hadn't been the first time so he knew the ropes. He had told a younger frightened prisoner that being in the slams was no different from being on the outside. He had to learn how to survive, fast!

After two months, Scully found himself walking out a free man. It was no big thing to him and dealing heavy in drugs for four years meant that his boss wasn't about to let him off the hook. As long as he didn't cross him, everything was cool. They had seen to it that Red got what was coming to him.

It was one of those rainy summer nights that brought a welcome relief from the summer's heat but frustrated everyone who had to drive through the rain slick streets. A '72 white Chevy wadded slowly through the flooded streets as the windshield wipers squealed loudly, trying to keep the windows free from the downpoor. It slowly splashed through the puddles in the parking lot of the fire station. A young white boy about twenty darted out of the car and between raindrops until he was inside the warm fire station. The rain had glued his shaggy blond hair to his face as beads of water trickled off each strand. The rain had changed the color of his short tan jacket as well as his jeans and sneakers.

Red quickly looked up from the desk as the boy rushed in. Downstairs was quiet since the men were upstairs watching the baseball game of the week. The kid looked like a college student as he shook the rain out of his shaggy hair. He had come for some scag, but Red insisted that he didn't know what he was talking about. His supply was low the night he set Scully up and the only reason he did it was because of the investigation of city employees. He knew he'd be a damn fool to lose that gig. So he had to turn informant when they closed in on him.

His only problem was that he was too dumb to

lay dead for a while. Even as the kid stood sopping wet and pressing him, Red began to rationalize. If this dude came out in all this rain for that little bit, then what the hell. He usually kept his supply in the lining of some books he kept in the bottom of his locker.

He remembered being low but there was more in there than he thought. His brain was so rattled that he didn't really think about how it got there.

Whatever he was going to do, he had to do it fast. The darkened hallway to the lockers was a few feet from the main desk. He cautiously walked to his locker, making sure no one was near. The squeaking door echoed as he tried to open it quietly. Once inside he knelt down and peeled back the cover of the top book. It only took a few seconds to scrape what he needed into a small manilla envelope and slip it into the pocket of his dark uniform. He felt his .32 behind the books, took it out and checked the barrels. He figured he better take it just in case the kid jumped bad. I'll just stick it in my pants, he told himself. He wasn't as nervous as the boy who paced the floor near the desk. But, just as the deal was made, the front door flew open, crashing against the wall. Three detectives and four cops stormed in as thunder clapped above the fire station.

Panic gripped Red as he reached for his heat. In

117

a split second the kid made his move. "Bam! Bam! Bam!" went the undercover agent's gun. Red was hit at such a close range that the force split his guts wide open, spreading the bloody contents all around him as he fell back against the desk. The syndicate had set him up to get Scully out but Red would never know that. And the fuzz had one less nigger to worry about.

Scully thought about that incident as the cab pulled away from the prison and headed toward the Social Club. As far as he was concerned Red deserved every damn bullet he got. There was no way in hell he would have lived because he had made his own plans about settling the score with Red. So, he didn't mind honkies doing his job for him! He just didn't like sitting in jail so long after Red's death. But the boss always had a reason for doing things. All that mattered to Scully now was that he was out and ready for action. He started to think about Carla when he realized what was happening.

"Hey, man!" he said sharply to the rugged looking white cab driver. "Where the hell you goin', man?"

The cab driver kept his eyes dead on the road as he turned at a traffic light. The sign AIRPORT flashed above Scully's head as he peered out the window.

"I said, where you takin' me, man?" he repeated. He leaned forward, gripping the back of the front seat.

The husky driver spoke in a deep voice.

"I got orders to take you to the airport. And orders is orders."

Scully pushed himself back in anger as he thought about what was about to happen. The rest of the ride was in silence while he tried to figure out what the hell was happening. Doing the cabbie in wasn't the answer so he'd just have to keep cool.

12 . . .

Scully watched the cool autumn breeze lift the Kentucky Fried Chicken bag in the air, reminding him that a good meal hadn't hit his stomach in months. Spicy ribs with greasy collard greens and a tasty spoon bread would have been more like it. He pushed back the sleeve of his wrinkled blue denim suit. The same suit he had on when he was picked up.

"Just eleven-thirty," he said. "Hmph. I wonder who Clara's screwin' now." She was still his woman and he didn't want no other nigger messin' with her.

The yellow cab pulled in a space between a 1974

sky blue Mercedes and a 1970 black Coupe de Ville. Scully leaned forward and looked out the window at the black haired olive-skinned white man sitting behind the wheel of the Mercedes. He couldn't figure out whether or not he had seen the dude before.

"There's a guy in that Mercedes waitin' for you," said the cabbie as he jerked his head to the left.

"I don't suggest you get no ideas, 'cuz there's a cat layin' for you and he's just fifty feet from here," the cabbie warned.

Scully sat on the edge of the seat and looked around slowly. If his neck could have turned 360 degrees it would have! All he could see was a packed parking lot and the sun peeping through the patchy blue clouds.

"You don't need to look for him," the driver laughed. "You just make the wrong move and your ass'll be his!"

Scully knew it could only be *them!* "What the fuck am I suppose to do?" he asked.

"Just get out and into that Mercedes. Betta' make sure you sit up front, *this time,*" he smirked.

Once upside his head is all I need thought Scully, but he just slid toward the door and opened it slowly.

"Don't worry 'bout payin'," said the driver.

"I wasn't," answered Scully sharply. "I like bein' chauffeured around by honkies too much!" he said sarcastically as he slammed the door.

He could see the cabbie's face turn red as he started the engine and backed off in a huff. Scully shook his head, getting the last laugh for a long time.

He turned the door handle of the plush Mercedes and realized that there was another gray dude in the back. Now he recognized the driver whom he had seen in a deal at the mill in May. But the car was something new.

He eased in cautiously, trying not to look too nervous. All the time he was checking out the two burly dudes as he felt his pulse picking up.

"Relax, Scully," said Parrini. "The boss figured you'd like a change of scenery."

"Well, I can dig it. But there's a whole lot I got to know first," he said. "Hey, ain't we met before?"

"Yeah," replied Parrini as he handed Scully the cigarette he had just lit.

"I thought so." He took a long drag that must have hit the bottom of his stomach before he let it out as a thin stream of smoke. He really needed more than a Kool but he had stopped mainlining when he started dealing in drugs. If other cats wanted to mess up their heads that was their business, but all he cared about was making that money and spending it like he wanted to. If he used it all in drugs he knew he'd be no better off than the dude in the streets. Sooner or later the steel mill days would end and if he didn't get all he wanted out of life while he was young he'd never get anyplace. He'd been supplying pushers and hadn't given anyone any bad stuff. That's why the syndicate trusted him. Too many deaths in the city might stir up some fires that they didn't need. He doubted that another nigger could have taken his place while he was in the slams. He hadn't been gone that long.

"Your chick's in Hollywood now as Carla Brown."

"Yeah, I keep callin' her Clara. Man, honkies got a bad habit of tryin' to make us into what they want! That's some jive shit," he said as he shook his head.

"Don't knock it, she ain't sufferin'!" he answered.

The dude in the back just leaned in the corner and said nothing. His heat bulged slightly under his coat but Scully wasn't even worried about that now that he felt no one meant to do him in.

"Why you talkin' 'bout her?" Scully asked with interest.

Parrini turned in his blue tweed suit. He was

123

definitely Italian and his dark eyes looked straight at Scully. Scully remembered how the movies used to make everyone think that only Italians were in the underworld. But Scully had found out a long time ago that its members came in many ethnic groups.

Parrini knew he didn't have much time so he had to get to the point.

"You'll be on a plane to L.A. in forty minutes. Don't worry about people. All that's been taken care of. We've even got a bag and a shirt and pair of pants in the trunk of the car for you. Just go into the john, change and get on that plane. When you get off take this key and open locker twenty-five next to the ladies room." He handed Scully the locker key and then lit a cigarette for himself. "There'll be a small bag with a .44 magnum, shells and some directions. Now the boss has gotten his feet wet in a few movie ventures. The government's about to change some tax laws on movie investments and the boss wants his foot in the door now before it costs him too much. So with Carla out there wanting to make it big he figured she'd be more than willing to jump at the chance."

Scully was beginning to fit the pieces together. He wanted to see Carla but he didn't want her to be used, too. He hadn't figured on getting her mixed up in this.

"She ain't gonna go for this," he insisted.

"*You're* gonna make sure she doesn't have any second thoughts. Look, nigger, we're giving you a choice if she backs out. A prison rap for the rest of your life or a pine box and no life!"

Scully wanted to blow both of 'em away. If he only had his trusty heat he'd damn sure have tried it. Nobody got the best of Scully! He yanked the key out of Parrini's hand but didn't say a word. The dude in the back slid across the blue leather upholstery until he was directly behind Scully.

"Don't worry, man. There's something big in it for you. Sooner or later they're gonna crack down on us in this city. There's no way a black mayor will let us operate like we want. And you're too valuable a man to wind up behind bars or even slaving back in the mill for the rest of your life. So, this is a big chance for you. Little black boy from Gary makes it big in Hollywood. Maybe even as a Hollywood producer. How does that grab you?" he smiled.

"It don't, honky! And don't plan on livin' if you call me nigger again!"

Parrini's smile turned sour. He had warned about Scully's hatred for whites. Even though he was cool with the Syndicate most of the men under the Lieutenant didn't push him too hard. Scully was the only nigger in town who could jump bad and

125

get away with it. That's because nobody dared to touch him without an order from the main man.

Once outside in the crisp Autumn air Scully grabbed the bag and clothes from the big guy. Parrini blew at Scully just as he passed the car and waved his plane ticket out the window.

"You can't go far without this, *Mr.* Scully," he sneered out the corner of his mouth.

Scully was one happy dude when Eastern's 747 Whisperjet landed safely at the L.A. International Airport. Even the roar of the engine was a welcome sound to his eardrums. Flying had never been his thing. If he couldn't travel in his hog, then he just wouldn't go. But, he didn't have much of a choice this time. Scully unclasped his seat belt like everyone else and eased his way into the line of departing passengers.

He passed the blonde flight attendant whose fake smile didn't do a thing for him. Opening locker twenty-five was all that mattered. Once off the plane and into the bustling lobby he moved through the waiting white faces and toward the lockers next to the ladies' room. He leaned forward and anxiously peered into the locker. There was the brown bag with a survival kit inside. It only took a slight lift and touch of the barrel with his strong brown fingers to know that a .44 magnum was inside.

126

One thing was certain. That .44 magnum was no joke. Scully had used it only once before in Chicago. He had just arrived home from 'Nam and stopped by a joint with some friends. Everyone was already high off reefers when his friend handed him a .44 for inspection. It was thought to be unloaded until he pulled the trigger and blew off a nigger's arm. That was the last time he had handled a magnum!

Since this was Scully's first time to L.A., he didn't want to look like a stranger. Instead, he went pimpin' down the passageway in his white, thin open-necked shirt and tight gray pants. He followed the signs leading to the baggage claim area as he gripped his small bag tightly. When the black American Tourister luggage slid down the shoot, he pushed his way between the two white men standing in front of him and started to leave the area until he was stopped by the guard. Once his bag was checked, he breezed out the door and hailed a cab.

Traffic was heavy for a Friday morning but the cab jutted in and out and headed toward the freeway. Scully looked back at the steel arches which crossed to what was known as the Theme Building. The palm trees stood tall as the warm sun drifted through the cotton clouds. It was the usual warm day for L.A. and a welcome change from Gary's

Autumn weather. Airplanes sounded like giant roller skates as they passed overhead.

"Say, man, how long will it take to get to where we're goin'?" Scully asked the Chicano cab driver.

"About twenty minutes," he answered in broken English.

Scully figured he wouldn't ask too many questions because he could barely understand what the dude was saying.

Instead, he lit a cigarette and ripped open the envelope that was inside the small bag. He knew he'd better follow instructions to the "T" or at least let them think he would. There was no way the white man could tell him what to do for long and sooner or later he'd beat his game.

Three typewritten pages were before him with instructions to burn after reading. This is damn near "Mission Impossible" thought Scully as he sifted through the pages. They knew he wasn't a dumb nigger. At least he could follow directions. It wasn't long before the cab's tires scraped against the curb in front of a stucco four unit apartment building off North LaCienega. The driver looked around and then stared strangely at Scully.

"Man, what's buggin' you?" Scully said in an evil tone.

"Oh, oh, nothing. It jus' that not too many blacks come to this section," the Chicano answered

128

with reservations.

"So, who says I'm black!" laughed Scully as he peeled off some bills that Parrini had placed with his ticket.

13...

The key to the apartment had been placed in the suitcase so there was no need to worry about contacting the resident manager. Scully hurried up the cement steps to the second floor and stopped at Apartment Four. He had to jiggle the key in the keyhole a few times before the door would open. He sighed in relief when he heard it click and open.

Once inside, he found himself in a small living

room that was only big enough to turn around in.
A red flowered couch and black leather chair with
a glass coffee table took up most of the room.
White curtains covered the narrow window and
the bare white walls and hardwood floors were just
as uninteresting. The rest of the one bedroom
apartment was much the same. At least the blue
velveteen bedspread gave the place a little class, he
thought to himself. Contact paper with a bold
brick pattern smacked him in the face when he
entered the kitchen. Even the black and white
kitchen set had been pushed against the wall to
give more space. They had stocked the refrigerator
but a broad grin flashed Scully's face when he saw
a half gallon of wine in a cabinet. As he glanced at
the clock to the right of the only window in the
kitchen he remembered that he hadn't set his
watch back. After doing so he poured a quick
drink, then showered and shaved.

Splashing on drops of Aramis reminded him that
Carla always liked to rub her body close to his
every time he wore it.

"Man, the boss thinks of everything," he told
himself as he sucked in a deep breath of the sweet
smelling cologne.

The urge to see Carla was building as he spread
his naked chocolate body across the bedspread. It
had been a long time since he held her or any

131

woman but he damn sure hadn't forgotten the pleasure it brought him. He knew he was wasting time but he was so mellow that he didn't see any harm in spending a few minutes daydreaming about screwin' his woman.

He drifted off into sleep and an hour later only the sound of two motorcycles revving up broke his sensuous thoughts. A quick glance at his watch and he realized that he had dozed off. Quickly he threw on a burgundy outfit and checked himself in the mirror to make sure he looked as good as he wanted to look. As soon as he slapped together a bologna sandwich, he stuffed it down his throat and headed straight for the front door. It was time to check out a few dudes and then he'd be with Carla.

Ben was yakking on the phone when a loud knock interrupted his conversation.

"C'mon in," he ordered as he continued to talk.

Scully entered the room with as much conceit as Fred Williamson. There was something about the tall black man in the doorway that made Ben take a second look. He sensed a familiarity that made him cut his conversation short. He didn't have to tell Scully to pull up a chair. By the time Ben hung up the receiver Scully was sitting down and lighting a cigarette.

"Always did like these leather and chrome director chairs," Scully said as he patted the arm of his chair.

"Well, I'm glad you do," Ben said with a serious look on his face. He got up slowly to give Scully the black power handshake but Scully didn't move. Ben looked like a fool standing with his arm extended. He drew his hand back quickly when he realized Scully wasn't going for any formalities.

"What is it that you want?" he asked as he walked around his long glass-topped desk. He sat on the end and folded his arms as Scully began talking.

"I'm Scully. Clara's ole' man."

It wasn't much of a surprise to Ben. He felt strong vibes when Scully walked through the door. There was more to not liking than a refusal of a handshake and now Ben knew what it was.

"I thought you were . . ."

"In prison?" Scully burst in. "Yeah, I was there and on a trumped-up charge. They finally let me out when they realized they had nothing to hold me on."

"So, what brings you to Hollywood?"

"That a jive-ass question," Scully replied with a mouth full of sarcasm. "Clara. Ah, Carla as you call her, is the only reason I'm here. She always wanted me to come out here with her but I couldn't see

further than the steel mill. I guess a few months
behind bars made me see what she was talkin'
'bout, so here I am. Besides, I got some big plans
for her. If I don't look after her nobody else will.''
He leaned back in the soft chair and pressed his
fingertips together as he spoke.

"What makes you think you're the only one
looking out for Carla?"

Scully had to think about that question for a
few minutes.

"Well, maybe somebody else is lookin' out a
little too much," Scully said with a smirk.

"Scully, I'm Carla's manager now. I will say that
she has had a few rough moments in her life but
she's made of tough stuff. She wants to be a star
and she knows that no one is going to give it to
her. It's just up to me to make sure she gets some
good deals and keep her head on straight."

Scully looked at Ben suspiciously. "And just
how close you been watchin' her?" Scully didn't
think Ben was too cool. He looked too much like a
"Negro" with more book learning than anything
else and he watched Ben as he eased off the desk
and went back to his comfortable chair.

"Man, I asked you a question!" Scully repeated
with force.

Ben still didn't answer and he could see that
Scully was getting pissed off as he squirmed in his

chair. He enjoyed watching "Mr. Ruff 'n Tuff" wait for an answer and he stalled him for a few more seconds.

"What you really want to know," he paused, leaning forward and placing his fingertips on the cold glass desk top, "is if I've been screwin' your lady.

"Damn straight!" Scully yelled as he jumped in Ben's face. "You damn straight!"

Ben just shook his head. It had been a while since he had to deal with a rough brother.

"Let me tell you somethin', Mr. College Graduate!" Scully said as he stuck out his chest. He pounded his mighty fist in his hand as he talked. "I'm a street nigger. That's right, a street nigger. I ain't no Ne-e-gro like you." He pointed his finger dead in Ben's face which caused Ben's eyes to widen. Scully couldn't keep still any longer. He didn't want to punch him, but if he had to he would. "Now, I didn't come out here to show my ass or jump bad with anyone, 'specially a so-called brother, but you betta get one thing straight. Ain't no book or no school in the world taught me how to deal with folks. I learned everything I know from the streets. There are cats that don't dig me for that but when I got to straighten out a dude I will and when I got to be cool and be a lover I can do that too! I ain't got no problems with none of it 'cause the streets taught me how to survive. And when that happens to a cat, it ain't nothin' 'bout wait and see how the other dude reacts. You just do what you gotta do. If you gotta punch him out, then that's what you gotta do. Even if you gotta kill 'em, then that's what you gotta do, too. Respect and survival, man! Respect and survival. Don't nothin' else matter. And just in case you forget another rule as folks in the ghetto live by, you betta listen closely before you get your ass kicked!"

By this time, Scully was dead in Ben's face. He could see that Ben was still as calm as a cucumber and that he hadn't ruffled him yet. Scully shook his finger as he talked. "Man, don't *nobody*, nobody mess with an man's ole' lady.' Nobody, you hear? 'Cause it's cuttin' time, man, it's cuttin' time!"

Scully unzipped a four-inch switchblade from nowhere and thrust the point dead against Ben's white shirt collar. If he had dared to move, it would have slid into his neck as smoothly as if it were slicing rare meat. Ben and Scully were about the same height. Even though Ben was bigger the pressure of that knife against his neck made him half Scully's size. All he could do was move back, stumbling into his padded chair.

"Man, you got me all wrong!" Ben yelled nerv-

ously. He had to come up with something fast
because Scully wasn't going to give him a chance to
say much more. His nerves were going haywire
inside his body. He couldn't help but tremble even
though he didn't want Scully to think that he had
the best of him.

"Just wait, man. Be cool! He made the mistake
of raising his right hand to push the knife away.
But Scully's moves were too fast as anger was
running wild. Scully's left fist bulldozed it's way
into Ben's gut, almost lifting him off the floor.
Ben's face twisted with pain as he fell against the
hard desk. Scully's size fooled him, but his punch
showed him who was top nigger.

Ben coughed like he was trying to cough the life
back into his body. If he held his gut any tighter,
he would have pushed a hole through his skin. But
he held on and breathed deeply to boot!

"It's not me you got to worry 'bout, man," he
whispered while he tried to catch his breath. He
laid back in the chair and flinched in pain. It had
been a while since he'd dealt with something like
this and as big as he was he realized that he had
come close to getting his ass kicked.

"It's Carla's agent, Brisco."

"Brisco?" Scully asked with a twisted face. "He
got her this last part didn't he?"

"Yeah," Ben was still trying to catch his breath

as he sat forward and loosened his tie. Scully stood above him with his knees locked and his arms folded across his body. He'd gotten the best of Ben and as long as Ben knew it he'd respect him.

"Well, what about Brisco? I know a little, but isn't his office next door?"

Ben nodded.

"C'mon, man!" Scully was irritated now because he hadn't gotten this bit of information.

Ben sat up in the chair as he fumbled for his cigarettes and lighter.

"Brisco was gettin' Carla some bullshit one-line walk-ons but she had to screw him, too!"

Scully was about to jump off the floor. "She had to what?? My Clara? Man, you jivin'! You know . . ."

"Cool it, man," Ben said as he raised his hands to calm Scully down. Scully couldn't do anything but pace the floor while Ben talked.

"Brisco told her that she had to do it if she wanted to get the parts. The girl you used to dig isn't the same chick now. She's changed because she thinks Brisco turned her into a whore!"

Scully slumped in the brown suede love seat at the opposite end of the room. His head couldn't take any more. He covered his ears in disbelief. His Clara thought too much of herself to stoop so low. Did Parrini know? he asked himself. He convinced himself that he probably did. Honkies ain't gonna squeal on each other! They're gonna stick together no matter what, he reminded himself.

"That bastard!" Scully roared. "I'll kill that motherfucker! Who does he think he is, messin' over *my* woman!" Fire spread across his eyes when he pounded his chest fiercely. "Why, I'll kill him!"

"Hold on, Scully. Right now we've got to think of Carla's career. We . . ."

"Career?" he interrupted in fury. "You *just* thinkin' 'bout her career? Why haven't *you* jacked his jaws by now?"

"Well, I . . ." Ben stumbled, "I didn't find out about it until the other day and that's when I suggested being her manager."

"Hmph! Niggers always late!" Scully was pissed off with everyone now.

Ben rose slowly in defense of himself. He paced the floor like a lawyer, pleading for his client's life. Only it was his own skin he was trying to save.

"I'm used to the games you have to play out here, Scully. Everyone is pullin' and grabbin'. Carla just got caught up in something she wasn't used to. She's got to pay her dues before she gets to the top. But it's business, that's all. We can't let her take it seriously. It's just business."

Scully was too pissed off to answer. His hands covered his face as he tried to fight the fire that raged inside him. He had to look calm even if he didn't feel calm.

"I've got Brisco under control now," Ben said as he stood above Scully. The threat of Scully's anger was fizzling out. "He won't abuse Carla now."

"Damn straight, he won't!" Scully got up slowly and walked over to the picture window that overlooked hazy Hollywood below. "I'm goin' to take care of this!"

"Wait a minute, man!" Ben had a suggestion. "Brisco ain't in now. So you can't get to him. Does Carla know you're here?"

Scully looked dead out the window at the moving traffic and shook his head while Ben talked.

"In about three and a half hours Les . . .oh, Les is the producer, and he's giving a cocktail party for the investors. It's a usual procedure but he wants them to meet Carla. Don't worry, Brisco'll be there. Les will be sending a chauffeur for Carla, so if you need a ride, I'll be by about six-thirty."

"Thanks man, but I don't need no ride," Scully answered.

Scully had cooled off even more as he thought of Carla. The thought of her filtered through his mind like a soft breeze.

"And Scully," Ben was even more relaxed as Scully turned to look at him, "don't start nothin'. Let Carla be the star . . . all the way."

By Bobbye B. Vance

Scully couldn't help but cough up a smile. Maybe Ben wasn't a jive dude after all. At least he could give him the black power handshake if nothing else. At least that was a starter.

14...

Narrow, winding roads lined with greenery and signs reading "DANGER, FOREST FIRES" led toward the sky and up into Beverly Hills, the home of the world's famous entertainers. Les' crib was a two story white brick with twelve rooms. It was on Summit Drive, not too far from Sammy Davis, and it had all the splendor of the movies.

The shrubbery that flanked the circular driveway was a forest green. Grecian statues and pillars gave another touch of class to the arched entrance.

The front of the house was all glass and even the water fountains in front of the windows looked as if they sprayed gold water. Tight security was a must as a high white brick wall and wrought iron fence kept out the gawking tourists.

Once inside, marble floors led everywhere while the glass chandeliers sparkled a shower of colors on glass tables and the Italian Provincial furniture.

The party wasn't the get down type that Carla was used to in Gary. Even the soft chamber music was a little too much to bear but no one seemed to notice. There were a few blacks sprinkled among the white investors, producers and those others involved with the film. But they were tripping out like everyone else, bullshitting about their pint-sized accomplishments in the industry.

Carla was a sharp contrast. She twinkled like a star in the sky in her tight black rhinestone-studded gown. Even though she had lost weight since moving to Hollywood, black made all her curves look round and full. It had taken her hair-dresser two hours to pile her dark wavy curls high and weave a string of sparkling rhinestones through each curl.

But she was together as she floated from one champagne sipping group to the next. Heads turned, eyes widened, and whispers grew louder. It was no big thing for Carla because she was the star, and they had come to drool over her. Even Joyce was there to join in the excitement.

"This is too much, Les," Carla giggled as she squeezed his hands affectionately. "I really owe you a lot."

Les smiled modestly as he planted a warm kiss on her soft olive cheek.

"You did it all, Carla. The tests and rehearsals have been great! All systems are go!" he raved. "Even Hank is pleased and he doesn't usually enjoy working with . . ."

"Beginners," moaned Hank, a mousy little black man who always wore a navy blue tam. Hank was Carla's director and somewhere in his career he decided to speak like white folks which made him more Negro than black.

"I detest working with beginners! They need so much coaching, you know. But a good director can bring out the best in anyone. Nevertheless, I must admit that it has been a pleasure working with you. You really aren't like the usual beginner." Hank flattered her and he could see that she loved it.

Carla leaned across Les and gave Hank an affectionate squeeze. She was much taller than him and his chin touched her breasts as she held him close. Hank had always tried to act professional but he was like a little kid being hugged by his mamma.

Ben even chuckled from across the room as he watched the two. Carla blew him a kiss while her other arm still hugged Hank.

Ben had walked in looking like a star himself. It

was obvious that his green tailored suit was made just for him. His 'fro looked like a wig with every strand in place.

Even Brisco wanted to steal the spotlight but no one would give him the time of day. Most people in the room knew about his reputation and knew that his days were numbered.

This was Ben's chance to get to Brisco. He squeezed his way between a small group of women and walked over to Brisco.

"Well, what ya' think, Brisco?"

"I'd say I've got a winner!" he boasted.

A black maid passed with a tray of sparkling champagne. Both men took a glass as she passed.

"That's what I want to talk to you about." Ben was ready to deal.

"Let's face it, man. You can't get Carla the roles she deserves."

"You tryin' to tell me I'm *not* a talent agent." Brisco knew he had been insulted.

"I'm tellin' you that you don't have the connections at Warners, Paramount, MGM, Universal or any place else. You can't get in any big door in this city." Ben towered over Brisco when he spoke.

"Now, you listen to me, Mr. Calder. A star like Carla doesn't come my way often. I've worked too hard for this and I'm not going to turn her over to you, that's for damn sure." He was determined that this black man wasn't going to mess up a good thing.

"You'll change your mind, Brisco. I'll see to it!" Ben was good and mean by now. Brisco was nothing but a chump to him and maybe Scully had the right idea.

"You better take you threats someplace else. You're wasting your time." Brisco didn't scare easily and especially by blacks.

Ben had to force his eyes away from Brisco but Les continued to call his name. He left Brisco with a silly grin on his face as he wiped the bottom of his wine glass.

By the time Ben got over to Les, an investor had joined them.

"Ben, I want to talk to you in private." Les insisted.

Ben was tired of talking but he knew he was a business man and he had to do it. He checked out the front door but there wasn't a sign of Scully.

Carla moved closer to Phil as everyone left. She sipped her wine slowly as he guided her to a couch in the corner near the terrace.

"Les is such a businessman. But we're delighted with his choice for a star."

Carla's thigh touched his leg as he moved closer to her. Phil looked like a Frenchman and was just as smooth. The scent of her perfume was running rings around his head.

"I just hope all of you are going to be as pleased when it hits the screen. I want it to be a smash! Nothing could make me happier," she sparkled.

Phil was just about ready to get to the point as he put his arm around Carla and rubbed her right shoulder gently. He could see that Carla wasn't too thrilled over his touch but she wasn't about to offend him.

"Well, maybe we need to make sure your bubble doesn't burst." His words caught Carla by surprise.

"What do you mean, Phil?" she said as she sat forward, twisting her neck awkwardly.

"This little gathering was set up to make sure we got a good look at our investment and . . ."

"Wait a minute," Carla whispered suspiciously. "What does Les have to do with this?"

"Oh, nothing. He's just concerned about dropping the check in the account. I know you've been through a hell of a lot, but this *is* your big chance and maybe your last!" he sneered.

Carla's heart dropped to her stomach. What shot was she headed for now? she thought nervously.

"Brisco tells me a lot of good things about you and let's say I'd just like to find out for myself."

"Brisco!" she slurred with disgust.

Phil nodded. "Yes, Brisco. So let's just go upstairs quietly."

No one paid much attention to both of them as they walked slowly up the winding staircase. It was a long walk to the bedroom at the end of the hall. Carla wanted to turn and run but she was too scared to resist.

"I can't believe this shit!" she said to herself as he forced her to strip. All she could see was a king-sized bed draped in satin. Her brown body looked sexier than ever against the white satin sheets. But Carla felt like garbage as Phil tied her wrists to the headboard. Again, her heart raced wildly, reminding her of the hours she had to submit to Brisco. But this was truly a freak. She wanted to kick him where it hurt the most but his slender hands grabbed her thighs every time she tried. She fought as long as she could but his small frame got bigger the closer he came toward her. Even closing her eyes couldn't blot out his flabby stomach as he pressed it against hers. She thought he would crack every rib in her body but the more she fought him the better he liked it! His filthy white sweat trickled in her eyes as he slobbered all over her.

"No, please don't!" she yelled as he rammed his two fingers between her slim thighs. "Keep your filthy hands off me. Keep 'em off!" she yelled.

"You know it's good to you. You know you like it. Don't fight me! I want you to be a star as much as you do," he panted.

He forced her thighs against the bed but she still wriggled and squirmed. They both slid with the silk, making him more excited. His tongue licked her breasts and then a trail of saliva covered her stomach. She wanted to vomit all over him. He sensed that she was ready to scream but as she opened her mouth a hard slap of his hand shut it. She'd been slapped by a honky before and wasn't ready for another bruising. She'd fought as hard as she could but nothing would work. He had forced her legs apart and had pinned her down. The fight within was collapsing to his strength. He was good and ready now. The pain darted to her throat as he entered her vagina. She moaned with anger every time he worked his way back and forth, deeper and deeper. She couldn't bear to look at the bastard. He was reaping with pleasure and she wasn't going to give him a damn thing! He'd have to take what he wanted and it felt as if he was scraping her wall apart. She was so damn sore. If she could only curl up in a knot, perhaps the pain would go away. But the bastard kept ramming it in until finally he came. His body fell limp as he soaked up his last bit of joy. He'd screwed a black woman and he'd never forget the pleasure it brought him.

Carla's tears couldn't phase him in the least. He had what he wanted and couldn't give a shit about her. The only thoughts that crossed Carla's mind was that she was still alive. The pain had made her body almost numb until Phil spoke.

"Don't quit so soon, Miss Star!"

The door flew open and two other white investors stood boldly in the entrance. "Let's let my partners get their money's worth," he growled.

"Jesus Christ," she whimpered. "Jesus Christ. I can't take it! I can't take it! Her black curls had fallen all over her shoulders and the rhinestones were all over the carpet. Her face was a maze of tears blurring her vision. It can't be! she sobbed to herself. It just can't be!

"Well, why don't you just turn over and let the boys give you a little pleasure from the rear?"

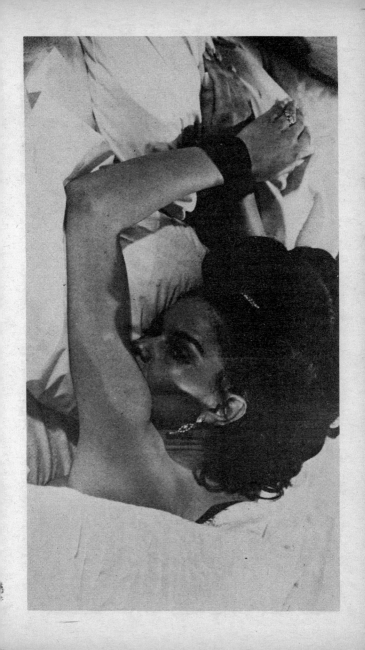

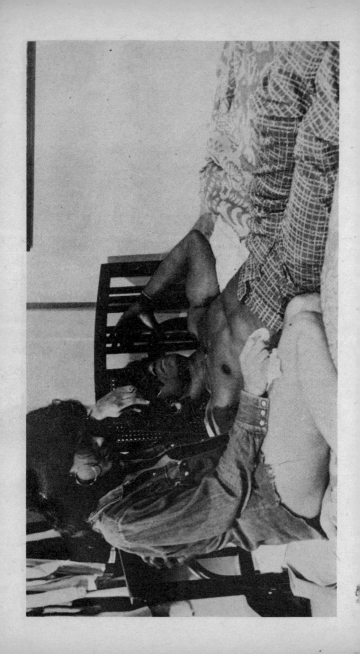

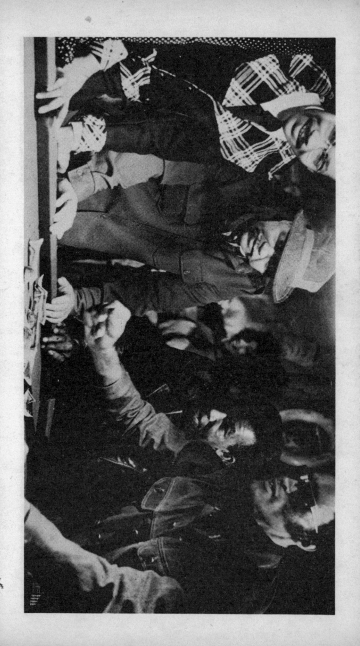

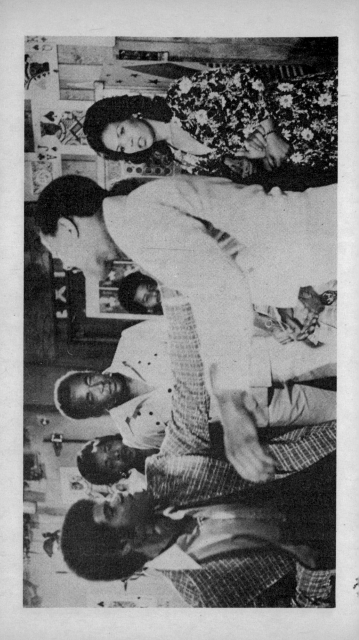

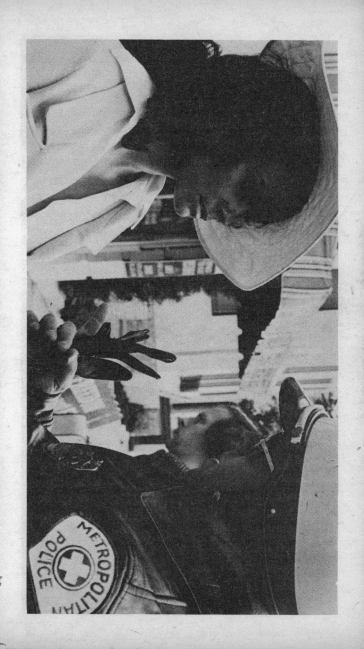

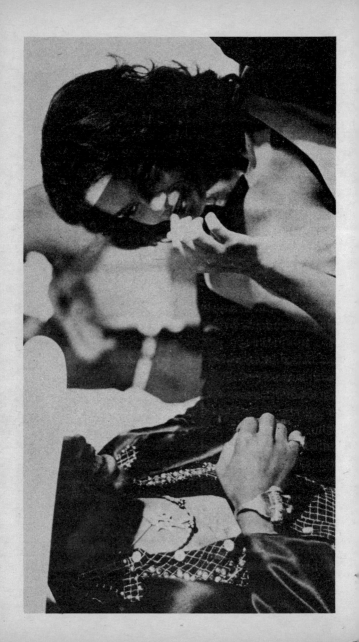

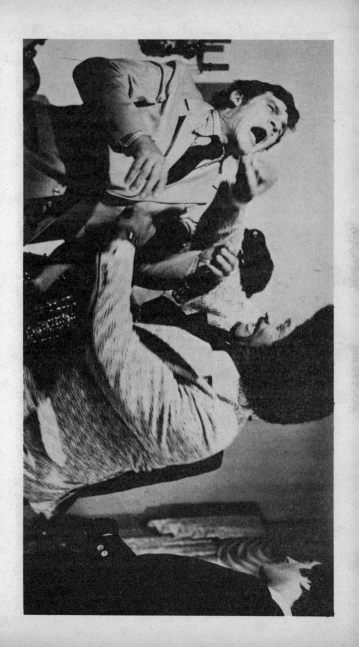

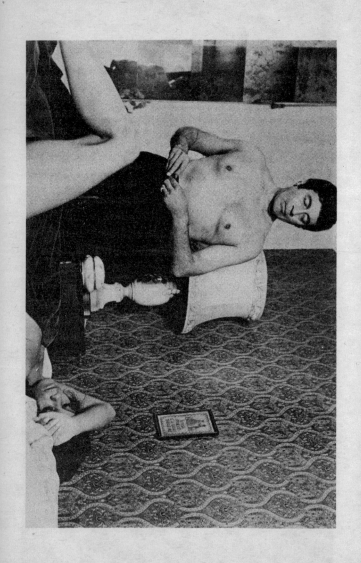

...15

The party was in full swing when Scully entered like a neon sign in his red suit with a ruffled white shirt and stocked heels. He was clean again! All eyes turned in his direction. Who was this dude, they asked each other. Ben went over to him immediately and introduced Scully to Les.

"Hey, man, where's Carla?" he asked anxiously.

"I don't know," Ben answered. "She's been gone about an hour now, hasn't she, Les?"

Les began to wonder as he looked at his watch.

"Say, you dudes aren't worried about her?"

Just then Carla appeared at the top of the stairs. She looked as if she'd been folded up in a trunk. It was hard as hell for her to hold her head up as she stumbled down the stairs. But she was determined to act like a star even if she didn't look like one. Even her hair flopped around her shoulders but she flung her head back.

"Ah!" gasped the onlookers.

And then a sudden hush fell across the room. Les was the first one to rush to the stairs before she collapsed.

Carla fought back the tears. If she had to look another white bastard in the face she thought she would vomit. Her body was numb so she gripped the railing for support.

"I've made sure your check will be at the bank on Monday morning, Mr. Producer." The words could barely reach the edge of her tongue.

"What are you talking about?" Les asked with a puzzled look.

"It seems as though Brisco wanted your investors to make sure they would get their money's worth and I . . ."

"Wait a minute, Carla," he said as he gripped her

shoulders. "I've had their money for over a week!"

"You've wh-a-at!" she screamed as she began to cry hysterically.

That was all that Scully needed to hear. He pushed Les out of the way and put his arms around Carla.

"Scully!" she cried in relief. "Oh, Scully, where'd you come from?" The tears wouldn't stop flowing.

"Baby, you don't have to take this shit from these motherfuckers no mo! They've all used you enough. Even Ben!"

"Now, wait a minute . . ." Ben blurted.

"No, nigger. You wait a minute! I know'd you was no good. Handin' me all that bullshit 'bout *business!* Business, my ass! You ain't black enough to manage no beautiful sister. You ain't even man enough! How'd you let this happen, man? Why, I oughtta split your ass wide open right now!" Every, evil vein in Scully's body popped into view. He made Ben look mighty small.

Scully cursed himself for not bringing his heat. The only reason he didn't was because Carla didn't like guns. It didn't matter, now. He was ready to square off as Ben stood helpless but he eyed Brisco slipping between the French doors that led to the terrace. He guided Carla to the bottom step then lunged toward Brisco.

It took him two seconds to get to him and when he did all hell broke loose. Both fists mutilated Brisco's body before he could raise a hand to protect himself. Fun and games were over once Scully tore into him. He didn't need any karate, just good solid blows to the head and body and one left jab that sprawled Brisco's bleeding body across the slippery marble floor.

Scully mumbled every swear he had ever heard as he pounded Brisco's head against the floor. He'd kill over Carla and he didn't care. Brisco's skull cracked against the marble, followed by a trickle of blood.

Ben and Les leaped toward Scully but they had all they could do to hold the wild grizzly bear.

"Call an ambulance, quick!" Les ordered as he held Scully's arms tightly.

Scully was fuming but Carla rushed over to calm him down.

"Easy, baby. I'm alright. Let's just get the hell out of here! C'mon, let me take him." she pleaded between tears.

The partygoers huddled in corners, not knowing when the shooting would start. Ben reluctantly turned Scully loose when he was sure of no more trouble. He knew he could have stopped a lot of shit before it had started but that was history, now. No one dared to move until Carla and Scully stumbled out the door to her limousine.

The spotlights along the driveway were a bright contrast to the darkness. Only the stars in the sky twinkled as the chauffeur slowly cruised toward Sunset.

After a long sudsy shower together, Scully and Carla held each other for comfort. It was only eleven-forty-five but the time change had Scully all confused. They talked for hours as Scully gently massaged the soreness out of her body. He wanted Carla but it would be a while before he'd get that close to her. Nothing came before his baby's well being.

It really wasn't the time to piss Scully off. The night had been a bitch for both of them and it wasn't the time to get evil. Besides, Carla knew she could call her doctor Saturday and have a prescription filled. Getting her hands on some bennies would be no problem. She had already decided that she would kick it after the first few days of shooting. Helping herself get over the hump was all that mattered.

Carla wanted a joint but Scully told her that he wasn't dealing in drugs anymore. Besides, he didn't ever want her messin' with nothing except his wine and cigarettes. She agreed to settle for both as he told her about his movie ventures.

"That's right, baby, I've got big plans for you. I'm gonna have my own movie company and you won't have to worry about none of this shit!"

They lay in darkness and only the music from the next apartment could be heard, reminding them of Gary. Just being close to each other relaxed them to the point where their minds were making love. It had been so long, but neither had forgotten how they used to really get down.

"Well, I've got to get through this one and I really don't think I can make it."

"Sure, you can," he told her as he held her smooth face in his hands. He kissed her moist lips gently, making sure not to put all his weight on her. She welcomed his touch. She wanted him to keep kissing her because it erased the nightmare she had just been through.

For the next few weeks of filming, Carla moved from Joyce's apartment to Scully's. He didn't think it would be too cool for her to just move in. At least, not yet. So she kept half of her things with him and left half with Joyce.

Scully's confidence wasn't enough for her. She had to take something to keep her up so she talked her doctor into giving her enough bennies.

The dressing room off Studio B wasn't as fancy as Carla would have liked it to be. The green cinder block walls reminded her of a traffic light, but the bright round bulbs around her long mirror reminded her that she was a star. Scully had sent a dozen long stem medium American Beauty roses that smacked a smile on her small, pretty lips. But the greatest satisfaction came from the bennies she popped before her first scene. By the time Hank knocked on her dressing room door she was ready to take on the world.

At the end of the first week, she knew that moviemaking was mighty damn hard work! Even the bennies weren't enough to keep her going. And when the second week rolled around she was ready for something stronger.

Carla stayed to herself because remembering lines was even becoming a chore. It was during Wednesday's lunch break that things began to change.

"Miss Brown," called a slim black lighting technician, the only one on the set. "Let me rap to you a few minutes."

Carla was drained from the last scene. She just wanted to get a few more pills! Everyone could tell by her eyes that she was on something. Carla rested her tired body against the frame of the door.

"I'm Andre. And, well . . . I just want you to know that I dig your work."

"Well, thanks," she said. It was the first real

compliment she'd heard in weeks.

"But, there's one thing that bugs me," he said as he rubbed his fingers across his bushy beard.

"What's that?" she folded her arms, bracing herself for the big letdown.

"You don't look like you're going to make it. Maybe you better eat more."

"Eat?" she laughed. She shook her head and started toward the dressing room.

"Food is not what's gonna keep me goin', brother."

"Then, maybe I can help." Andre caused her to stop dead in her tracks. He had what she wanted and he knew it.

"Can I come in your dressing room for a second?" he whispered.

Carla didn't see any harm so she let him follow her inside and pointed to a wooden folding chair in the corner. Andre refused to sit but leaned against the dressing table when she sat down.

"Sister, speedballin' will do it for you," he guaranteed.

Carla's eyes got big as headlights.

"I'm hip," she assured him, "But, ah, I ain't goin' that heavy." She knew that getting high off cocain and heroin was no joke. "Now, I just need a few more bennies and that'll do it." She looked around the top of her dressing table as she talked, searching for the pills.

"I know I had a few here, somewhere." Her trembling fingers fumbled through the drawers, her pocket book and all around the floor near her dressing table. She sighed in relief when she found the plastic in her make-up bag.

"Whew! That's all I need. I've got . . ." her voice trailed off when she saw two pills. Now that would never make it, she thought to herself. Her eyes met Andre's and their minds were one.

"If you weren't on the set, I'd swear *you* threw the rest of these out." She knew damn well that she had had more.

"Wow, sister, don't start accusin' me. Man, anything could have happened. I ain't forcin' the stuff on ya. But, if you want it, I got it!" He knew he had her. The smirk on his face let her know she wasn't messin' with a kid.

Knock! Knock! Hank was on the other side of the door. "Ten minutes, Carla."

Andre and Carla froze until the footsteps trailed off.

She bit her lip as she gazed nervously at Andre. He pushed his wire-rimmed glasses up on his nose and put his hands on his hips with confidence.

"Well, what you gonna do?" he asked again. "I got it right here in my jacket pockets." He patted his leather jacket. "Better make up your mind."

Scully would kick her ass, she thought, but Scully wasn't there now and he'd been barred from the set as a result of the fight at Les' pad. He'd never know. Anyway, she'd kick it in a few days.

"Okay, Okay," she said hurriedly as her eyes glanced quickly from Andre to the door and back to Andre again. "But I can't speedball. Heroin wouldn't give me the high I need and snortin' coke, well, it wouldn't last long enough."

Andre began to think. "What about speed?"

Speed would do it, she thought to herself. That would do it just fine. She nodded her head excitedly. She knew enough about speed to make it.

Andre pulled out a small manila envelope. "This should do it," he said as he handed it to her. Carla ripped the envelope open and peered inside at the little white pills. She sighed in relief as her long nails scooped them up.

"How much do I owe you?" she asked, looking for a glass of water.

"You don't owe me a dime."

His words caught her by surprise.

"What's that mean?"

"Let's just put it this way," he said, turning the doorknob, "I'm the only nigger behind those cameras. Maybe I'm just a technician but I wanna keep this gig. Now, I figure like this. A good word from you will keep me here. You dig?" he smiled.

By Bobbye B. Vance

Carla nodded. She knew it was rough for blacks to get jobs in the industry and she needed him as much as he needed her.

"I dig," she said as he opened the door.

16...

Weeks passed and everything was mellow. Carla was performing like a star. She was so hyper that she surprised herself.

Scully was forced to deal with his own business and since Carla was working long hours, he saw very little of her. Flying back and forth to Gary took up most of his time. Parrini had orders for him to get it together, now that Carla was wrapping up her first film.

Brisco was forced to give up Carla. Dealing with Scully got to be too much. Now that Ben was her manager, he spent more time with her and he could tell a change had taken place. She was hard, not the bright-eyed girl he first met.

It was the last day of filming and Carla thought she'd be ready to celebrate, but instead she felt drained. She had tried to stay off speed but found she still needed it to keep her going.

Carla and Ben sat in the screening room waiting for Les to view the day's rushes. He couldn't take his eyes off her as she kept changing her position in the cushioned theatre seat.

"What's with you, Carla?" he asked.

"What's with me?" she laughed. "Don't you know? I've sweated my ass off for all of you. You've used me up. Just like the song says! And I didn't ask for this. I'm a star! Hmph! I had to lose Clara Brown to do it. Even when I look in the bathroom mirror I stare like hell, tryin' to find a trace of her. But, I can't find her, Ben. I can't find her," she frowned. She crossed her legs so that she was looking dead at Ben. The light in the projector room behind Ben and Carla flicked on which caused Ben to take a quick look over his shoulder. Carla impatiently twisted in the cushioned theatre seat. She wondered what was keeping Les.

"Where the hell is Les?" she mumbled.

Ben just shrugged his shoulders.

"He's getting like you and Brisco," she slurred.

Ben cut his eyes at her. He almost felt as if it was time to duck from all her insults.

173

"Greedy!" she said as the door to the screening room squeaked open. She patted Ben's hand as he placed it on the arm rest between them. "Don't worry, honey, Mama's learned a big ole' lesson—and especially from Brisco. And that's if you want something in this big raggedy world, you betta' take it, 'cuz nobody's gonna give you shit, let alone care about you! And white folks don't care about niggers! They don't care that I've got talent. All they see is dollars. When I first met you, you told me when I get on top I could call the shots. Well, I'm almost there and you can bet your ass, that's just what I'm gonna do! And let me tell you somethin' else. As much as I can't stand the ground Brisco walks on, I'll give him credit for one damn thing."

"And what's that?" Ben grunted.

"He takes what he wants and that's the only way you can make it in this lousy world!"

"You've really learned the ropes."

"I've learned it the hard way, buster!"

"Well, now that the film is over, you must really feel like a star. The critics are saying you're the best black actress on the horizon."

"Hmph! I don't know what I'm best at. I thought I'd be ready to celebrate. Scully's not in town and there's nothin' else for me to do except go back to Joyce's . . . alone."

Ben laughed. "If things were better between us, you know you could . . ."

"I could go home with you no matter what! As long as it dealt with *business.*"

"Hold on, Carla, we started out as friends, remember? And . . ."

Carla butted in, "And things were cool until Scully came and saved me, if you really want to know!"

"Lady, you're on top now. But don't forget you got to fight like hell to stay there. And, you better make sure you got someone to fight for you! The rate you're goin', you won't be there long!"

"Well," broke in Les as he leaned over to kiss Carla. "Am I interrupting something?"

"No," said Ben cunningly. "I was just congratulating Carla."

"Yes, you really deserve it, dear," Les said, squeezing her shoulder as he sat behind her. "Oh, by the way, Carla, I'll expect you in my office early tomorrow," Ben added.

It was nine-thirty p.m. when Joyce's phone rang loudly. Carla had just come in.

"Who?" Joyce asked.

"Oh, Scully," she said flatly, "hold on." She yelled up to Carla's bedroom, "Pick up the phone, Carla. It's Scully, long distance."

"Hey, baby!" she yelled. "When you comin'

home?" She pulled off her dress and bra while she talked. She was let down by his answer. "Everyone has to take care of business! Doesn't anyone want to enjoy life?" She paused again and threw herself on the bed.

"Sure, you know I'm gonna do the picture. But what about Ben? This is legit, isn't it?"

Scully mumbled again.

"Look, Scully, Ben's a pain in the ass, but he is my agent now and he is straight. I just hope that you know what you're getting into. There ain't too many blacks with companies. It just ain't easy."

Scully reassured her that everything was cool.

"I don't know, baby. Les really wants to tie me up for a few more pictures and... What? Now, wait, baby, I'm thinkin' 'bout your future, too! This shit isn't easy and since I've made a stab at it, and doin' damn well, let's leave well enough alone. What?" she paused again. "You *are* a man. Look, I'm gonna keep workin'. This is my life. You just take care of my needs and everything'll be cool. What? Okay. If you really want to be a filmmaker, we'll talk about it when you get back. Look, I haven't been sleeping much lately and Ben wants me in his office early. Today was the last day of shooting and I wanted to celebrate with you. But, I guess I can wait until tomorrow. You should be home when I leave Ben's so I'll call you. Now don't disappoint me, baby." The phone slipped from her hands. All she could do was crawl up like a ball and catch some z's. Joyce had suggested going to a gig but Carla was knocked out.

It was twelve-fifteen when Carla dragged in wearing a blue denim suit. Her hair was pulled back and a blue scarf held it tightly.

She acted as if everyone was late but her.

"I'm glad you're all here," she said impatiently as she plopped down in the chair. Ben and his assistant, Mel Michaels, looked right through her.

"My, my," she said in a high voice. "This is what I call a welcoming committee!"

"You're late, Carla." Ben was cool. He knew she was going to be pissed off anyway so there was no need to make it worse.

"Well, I don't usually get a chance to sleep late," she said as if an excuse would help.

Ben shuffled papers back and forth as Carla bubbled on.

"What's up, Ben?" she asked. She grabbed a cigarette from Ben's desk and sat on the opposite side of Mel. Then she impatiently waved her cigarette in the air as if ordering someone to light it. Since Mel was the closest, he accepted being her flunky.

Five minutes had passed before Carla stopped bragging about herself.

Ben's head shook in disbelief and he had just about tuned Carla out but a few words here and there caused his ears to perk up. He slid the legal documents in front of Mel for him to read and sign. Mel was so chubby that he grunted loudly as if it was needed to turn his body sidewards in the brown leather armchair. His eyes skimmed across the papers, then he raised his arm to sign.

"Well, what's all this about?" asked Carla as she pointed across Mel and at the papers.

"Carla, Mel is handling everything from now on," Ben said coolly, never raising his head.

"What?" she yelled in disbelief.

"He'll handle all business and any other needs you might have. Just sign right here." Ben had his shit together!

Carla's mouth was wide open while she watched him walk around the desk and toward her with a handful of papers. He could see that she was getting ready to explode.

"Don't put on a scene here, baby. There aren't any cameras. Besides, you'd be wasting your time."

"But, Ben!" she whined, "I need you out there for me!"

"I said cut the crap," he ordered. "I'll still be reviewing everything for approval but I've got other clients who demand my attention."

"Demand your attention!" she flared. "I

demand your attention!"

"Not anymore, Miss Brown. Now sign, please." Ben had his shit together and as Carla sat smoldering he looked at her calmly. All the days and nights they had spent together seemed so far in the past. It wasn't easy for him to accept the change in her but he had.

"You've gotta listen to your agent and you don't listen to anyone except Scully."

"Oh, now it's Scully, is it?" she said as if she resented Ben blaming him.

"He's not the only one who's turned you into a bitch. You've done it to yourself!"

She was about to tear into him but realized that it was hopeless. Ben was a shrewd businessman and nothing she could say would change his mind as the papers slipped out of his hands into hers. Then Mel slowly handed her a pen.

"Mel, it looks like you and I are going to have a long life together," she said as she scratched her name across the documents. He didn't know what to say about the whole scene, so he just forced a nervous smile.

"So, let's get started *rat* now! I feel like a shopping spree coming on. A star needs to keep up that image, so I deserve a new wardrobe, a mansion, and even a Jaguar!" She threw the papers on Ben's desk and stormed toward the door.

"I don't have all day, you know!"

Mel followed like a St. Bernard on a leash.

"And as for you *Mr.* Calder, you'll be dealt with later!"

... 17

The sun disappeared behind the palm trees and a cool breeze gripped the air when Scully burst into Ben's office. Scully's grand entrance didn't phase Ben in the least.

"What's this shit about you turnin' Carla over to another honky!" he blasted.

"Man, news travels fast!" Ben answered calmly. Ben could look at Scully's light green jacket and see that he was carrying his heat. A wild bull was standing in front of him and he had to keep his cool.

"I thought you were out of town," he said as he put on his navy blue jacket.

"I was, but I had just got in when Carla called

me and told me about this morning."

"Well, then there's nothing else to say," answered Ben as he started toward the door.

"Hold on, Jack!" Scully grabbed his arm, causing him to stop in his tracts. He broke his hold, but Scully whipped out his .44 magnum.

The size of the gun popped Ben's eyes out.

"I ain't got a lot of time. So you get over there and change them damn papers, now!" Scully was ready to do him in. Parrini had warned him before he left Gary, and he knew that things had to go smoothly now more than ever or his ass would be theirs!

"Now just cool it, man!" Ben's voice was getting louder. He knew that Scully was crazy enough to blow his head clear across the room so he had to talk fast!

"I don't know what else Carla's been tellin' you but you better get a good look at that chick. Either she's jivin' you or you're behind this shit!"

"And what's that 'spose to mean, man?" Scully asked as he gripped the gun.

"It means that she's not the same person she was when she came out here. It means that when it came time to get in front of those cameras, she couldn't do it. Her mind and body had been so fucked over that she didn't have anything but hate left in her. By that time she'd lost all confidence in herself. Even your being here screwed her up. Yeah, she digs you, but her career comes first. So she's had to build up her confidence and not let anything stop her. What I'm really trying to get across to you, Mr. Scully, is that she's been poppin' pills to get through that flick!"

"What!" Scully exclaimed in disbelief. Not *his* woman! She wouldn't dare mess with nothing, he thought.

"You shittin' me, man?"

Ben shook his head. "No, man. She went from bennies to speed." He could see that he had Scully now and the threat of being killed wasn't as great.

Scully's mind was on Ben's words as he slowly put his gun down and slumped into the nearest chair. A defeated look splashed on his face while he shook his head in disbelief.

"Where'd she get it from?" he asked as he stared out at the smog-filled sky. He had all he could do to fight back tears. It was one thing to know about others getting strung out, but he couldn't deal with his old lady getting into it.

"I think I know, but it doesn't matter. She can get anything she wants, anywhere." Ben walked over to Scully. He towered over him as he watched Scully bury his face in his hands.

"Look, man, she won't listen to me and she'll blow her career at the rate she's going. If you don't help her, nobody can!"

"Hmph. If I don't help her! I thought I *was* helpin' her. I got her future all mapped out and yours, too. But, I don't know, now."

Ben gently touched his shoulder.

"Man, I know how you feel. She means somethin' to me, too. But you're her nigger. You gotta do it."

Scully's heart sunk so low that he felt it in his stomach.

"I need to kick her teeth in!" he suggested as a spark of anger burst in his veins.

"Naw, man," said Ben as he sat across from him. "Maybe, you better stay away from her a few days. You're too up tight now. Besides, she thinks she can kick it. No, it'd be best to just call her. I'll have Joyce keep an extra eye on her."

Scully sat motionless for about ten minutes, then rose slowly. Ben's eyes followed him but he didn't get out of his chair. Scully didn't look at him. Instead, he stuffed his .44 in his holster.

"Ya know, you might be an okay dude after all. I can't seem to kill ya', yet." He dragged to the door and opened it. Ben watched him leave with saddened eyes but sighed deeply when the door shut tightly.

Scully kept his promise and phoned Carla every

By Bobbye B. Vance

night. His body was aching to hold her but he'd
have to wait a little longer. Late Wednesday night
he called, saying that some last minute business
had come up and he had to fly to Gary. Carla was
pissed off. She'd planned to spend the weekend
with him, just screwin' and partyin' but all this
business was messing up her plans. All she could do
was pop a few more pills and say the hell with the
world.

For the next two weeks, *Variety*, *Hollywood
Reporter* and all the top fan magazines were raving
up the new black star, Carla Brown.

One moonlit Thursday night, Carla and Joyce
danced in a sea of newspapers, magazines, and
telegrams. Carla's sheer pink negligee was covered
with a blanket of clippings.

"Look! Look!" she screamed with excitement.
"They're saying that this is going to be the
biggest premiere to hit Grauman's since Marilyn
Monroe's days. Ain't that some shit?" She kicked
her legs in the air when she sprawled over the soft
oriental rug. "Oh, oh, I can't believe it!" She
grabbed a handful of telegrams. "And even Gary,
Indiana remembered me. Home folks!"

Joyce screamed along with Carla as she laid on
the floor sifting through magazines.

"Gosh, Carla! This is too much! And wait until
the public sees you. If this happens for a sneak

185

preview, girl, you'll floor 'em at Grauman's!"

"Joyce, I really didn't like playing the karate queen rough 'n' tuff type," she said as she jumped up to a karate stance. "Next time I'm going to be a sweet, innocent school girl who falls in love with a married man." She winked. "I think I'd like that."

Joyce laughed. "Well, I could think of something better but you do your own thing!"

The phone cut their laughter. Carla hopped up and grabbed it.

"Hello-o," she said in a sultry voice. "Scully! Hey, baby! You should see the telegrams from home. I'm a star, baby, a star!"

Scully was quick and to the point.

"What? Yeah, I'll get ready. Bye," she answered, then hung up.

"What's up?" Joyce asked, thumbing through the telegrams.

"Scully is ready for me. Can you dig it!"

Scully was rapping at the door thirty-five minutes later. Carla raced down the stairs and out the door yelling to Joyce on the way.

She didn't see the nervous look in Scully's eyes. All she saw was the man she had been waiting to hold. Her body pressed against his as she pressed a kiss on his big brown lips. He held her tightly, rubbing his hands across her tight denim jeans. They stood beneath the star-studded sky wrapped in each other's arms.

"Say, woman," he rubbed his hand along her side, "you feel like you could use some meat on them bones."

Carla looked down at her thin body.

"Well, I've still got curves, but I guess I could use something to eat. Eating hasn't crossed my mind lately." She clung to Scully as they bounced down the stairs and into the cool air. He held the door open for her, then, after shutting it tightly, he walked around to the driver's side.

"It ain't like my hog, but it will get me around," he said. "In about a week, I'll have mine shipped here."

"Don't worry," she waved her hand in the air, "I've ordered a sky blue XJ6 that you can have whenever you want!"

"Naw, mama. Gotta have that diamond in the back with the sun roof top!" They both laughed. "Can't be leanin' on no eleven miles to a gallon of gas!"

"Well, your ride doesn't get much more," she reminded him.

"I'm hip. But at least I don't have to send to England to get no damn parts!"

"But you must remember, baby," she said in a sexy voice. "I'm a star and a star doesn't worry about how much anything costs!"

"Well, how come you don't buy a Rolls?" he asked sarcastically.

"I'm saving that for when I get an Emmy. Let the studio buy it for me!" They sat laughing and kissing until Scully cut acting a fool.

"What's wrong, Scully. You stopped laughing."

He slumped behind the wheel and rubbed his hands across his face. Carla looked puzzled when she saw him rest his head on the back of the plastic seat.

"You sick, baby?" she said, spreading her fingers over his large shoulder.

"No. I ain't sick. But you are," he whispered with his eyes closed.

"Me?" she said as her body stiffened. The bright lights from an approaching car made her turn her head for a moment.

"What do you mean, me?" she asked again.

Scully told her about his bursting into Ben's office, ready to do him in until he told him that she was using speed.

Carla put on a big dramatic scene, trying to deny it, but Scully yelled at her, stopping that shit then and there.

"I ought to slap the shit out of ya' but I don't wanna mess up your face!" He was pissed off again.

"Scully. You wouldn't?" she gasped.

"Look, I told you back in Gary. Don't start that crap! Have you looked at yourself lately. Well . . . have you?"

Carla hung her head in silence.

"Well, take a good look, Carla, take a look!" His large hand reached over, grabbed her chin and shoved it in front of the rearview mirror before she knew what was happening.

"Ah-h!" she squeaked when her nose hit the mirror. Scully let her go, causing her to hold onto the glove compartment for support.

"I'll knock every motherfuckin' tooth out of your head if I ever catch you messin' with that shit again. Now, I told Ben I'd stay away from you for a while and I did. But I'm back and I'm still pissed off. I don't know what you'll be freakin' off on next. If it means that you can't shit without my being there, then that's the way it's gonna have to be. I got too much tied up in you and you're not gonna throw your life away. You dig?"

Carla nodded as she wiped her tears. Her nose was running and she sniffed as if she couldn't stop.

"Stop that damn cryin' and sniffin'!" Scully banged his fist against the steering wheel. Yelling at Carla made his blood boil. He was angry, but to blow off at a woman, and especially his woman, just wasn't his thing. He felt sorry for her but he had to come on strong.

189

"Can you kick it?" he asked, looking at her. It was dark inside the car but he could see the tears glistening down her cheeks.

"Yes," she whimpered. "I haven't had any in four days. I felt a little sick, but I think I can hold out."

... 18

Only the sound of the police siren in the distance could be heard as they sat in silence. Scully reached over. He felt her sadness in the pit of his stomach and something pushed him toward her. Her wet tears fell over his lips as he kissed her cold cheeks.

"I'm going to get you somethin' to eat, then we'll talk. There's a hamburger joint across from the Bantam Cock. We'll stop there and then go to my place."

Carla couldn't move. All the life had left her as they headed toward West LaCienega. Scully was right, she thought to herself. He had to be strong for himself and her, too.

By the time they got home, they were full and ready to get some sleep but Scully knew he had to have her.

The bedroom was cluttered with clothes and his packed suitcase.

"Looks like you need a woman's touch," she suggested.

"I'm hip," he laughed. "But, we'll just push these things on the floor, like this and worry about it tomorrow. Right now, we've got some sho' 'nuff business to take care of!"

Scully had to get her to sign the papers Parrini had given him and he knew it had to be tonight. But, she looked so good to him that he couldn't take his eyes off her body. He guided her slowly to the soft king-sized bed and pulled her tight jersey over her head. Her long hair fell over her face exciting him even more. When she unzipped her jeans, his strong brown hand gently slipped around her waist to help her slide them to the foot of the bed. They fumbled out of their clothes until their naked bodies were locked together. Every inch of her was relaxed for the first time in two months. Her pointed nails dug into his muscular back and he moaned with pleasure. She used every trick she knew to excite him and he ate it up!

"Honey," he moaned, "Don't stop. I need you so damn much!" He flooded her body with hot

192

kisses, causing her to squirm with excitement. She moaned and groaned, knowing that he was getting hard. Her legs locked around his thighs, welcoming his every move. Their breathing grew louder as they rolled across the wide bed. They hadn't even stopped to pull back the blue velveteen spread. There wasn't any time for small stuff. Carla was ready to burst but she held on until her man was ready for her. And he came, just like she wanted. The weight of his body made her feel oh, so real, so much like a woman. Scully was a lover, again. The man she knew and loved was drowning in her arms and she was there to save him, to love him, and give him all that was in her.

"I love you," she whispered. "I love you, Scully. Please don't leave me again," she pleaded.

Scully wasn't going to leave her again. Just being with her made him remember the good times they had together in Gary. His nose rubbed against her chin while his heart raced with satisfaction.

"I won't leave you, honey. Right now, I just want to lay here and feel you." He knew he could get it up again and she'd be ready.

"Just hold on to me. I ain't through yet," he smiled then planted a kiss on her neck.

His hot breath added to the heat that he had aroused in her. She couldn't move if she wanted to. Just knowing that he wanted as much of her as he could get satisfied her for the moment. Shit yeah! she thought to herself. I'll wait for you, forever, whenever. Just treat me right and I'll be your woman.

By the time they got out of bed, the sun was lifting from the apartment houses and palm trees in the distance.

Scully's arm was sprawled across Carla's breasts and his matted 'fro rested comfortably on her shoulder.

"Hey, what time is it?" she said, clearing her throat. She tried to raise her head but gave up when she realized Scully had her pinned down. He kissed her cheek softly and raised his head to check out the clock on the dresser.

"Holy shit!" he said, remembering the papers. "Look, baby, we got to get up. There's some business we gotta take care of."

"What business?" her breasts shook as she braced herself on her elbows.

"I got some papers here." He scrambled out of bed and into his briefs.

"Just let me get them out of my case." He turned around and shuffled through his case that was in the corner near the window.

"Here, baby." He sat next to Carla and kissed her lips softly. "Just look these over."

Carla frowned as her eyes skimmed the printed

pages.

"Who's Mass Productions, Inc.?"

"That's my company," he bragged.

Carla squinted as she looked at him squarely.

"Scully, where did you get enough bread to have a film company?"

Scully searched for a butt.

"What you mean?" he asked, finding a pack on the bedstand.

"You heard me!" Her voice got louder. "Nigger you ain't got that kind of bread and I *know* you don't have it!"

"Okay. I got some backers, but it don't mean nothin'. We're gonna have plenty of dough."

Carla didn't want to sign it and she shook her head wildly.

"Naw, Scully. I ain't goin' for this! I don't know what I'm getting into."

She threw the papers on the bed. He was ready to cop a plea. He had to make her sign it or else Parrini would be rapping on his door.

"Please, baby. Just sign the papers." His hands shook as he gathered them up. "Please."

"You're not telling me everything. Are you tryin' to get out of a jam?"

"No." His voice cracked when he talked. "What makes you think that?"

"You've never acted like this before," she

paused and threw her legs over the edge of the bed. After she dressed, she quickly reached for the cigarettes.

"I think I better talk to Ben. He's pretty pissed off at me, too. But this is business and . . ."

"Ben already knows you'll be signing for this flick. In fact, he thought it would be a good thing. I'm going to get with him on Monday," he lied.

"Ben said that?" she asked in disbelief.

"Damn straight!"

Carla reached for her pocketbook to find her comb then strolled to the mirror and began combing her dark hair.

"I still say I gotta think this over, Scully. You better take me back to Joyce's. She's 'spose to take me to sign papers on my house."

Scully hadn't heard anything except "think over" and "home." Putting all his shit on the table wouldn't be too cool, he thought. But, if he didn't, he'd still be in a fix.

He sucked in a deep breath of air and slapped his thighs.

"Okay, you're the boss. Black women always get their way," he smiled, trying to amuse her.

"This doesn't have a damn thing to do with gettin' any way. I just gotta do what's best for me. Shit's happenin' so fast that if I don't plan I'll lose everything I got!" She turned and walked toward

By Bobbye B. Vance

Scully.

"You look so down, baby," she said softly as she sat next to him and kissed his shoulder. "Put those papers away for now and tonight we'll talk about it again."

"It may be too late!" he said through clenched teeth.

"You've got me puzzled," she answered. "But, we'll get it together later. Right now I got to go, so get that 'fro together and let's split."

Friday morning's traffic on the freeway was heavier than usual but Scully managed to weave his way in and out. By the time he got back to his apartment, pains had grabbed his stomach.

"I betta get some chow," he said, holding his belt buckle.

The documents had never been put away and Scully didn't need for anyone to get his hands on them. He always kept his dough on him.

Once inside the apartment, he looked around to make sure everything was like he left it.

"I better get myself together and stay out of this crib for awhile," he thought to himself out loud.

After he had hopped in the shower, he got clean again in a denim outfit. Getting the documents together and packing his .44 were on his mind.

R-r-ring! R-r-ring! R-r-ring!

"Now who in the fuck is that?" he asked himself. His hand grasped the receiver but he didn't pick up the phone. "If that's Parrini, I don't need to talk."

Something inside told him not to pick it up. So he paced the floor nervously while it rang.

"Looks like I better make the rest of my connections. Where's my book?"

He scrambled through his suitcase and found his brown address book.

"Duz, Duz. Where is that dude?"

He found the name of a cat who used to hang out at the Social Club and always bragged about moving to L.A. They'd been tight and Scully knew he could count on him.

... 19

By nightfall, Scully had gone to Duz's pad and mapped his plans. His tires screeched wildly as he pulled into the curb in front of his apartment. Later, when he returned to his own neighborhood it was unusually noisy with record players blasting in every direction. He would just run up and get his rags and split to Carla's pad.

As he dashed like an Olympic runner, his feet barely touched the steps. The key jammed in the lock, but he messed with it a few seconds then stopped suddenly. A sense of danger flashed through his head. He'd be a fool not to go in ready, he thought. With the .44 in his right hand, nothing could keep him from doing what he had to do. The click of the key opened the door and Scully was smothered in darkness. Once his eyes adjusted to the change in light, he peered around the room cautiously. His hand patted the wall in search of the light switch.

Scully's heart was beating as loud as the music in the other apartments.

There damn sure was someone in here, he realized quickly. He had a habit of moving around in a darkened apartment. In case he had to shoot his way out, he'd have the advantage.

Once his hand was away from the light switch, he eased along the wall, feeling every rough spot. He moved in the opposite direction of the couch, counting every step, moving slowly, slowly toward the narrow hallway. His ears and eyes were as sharp as a hawk's. A shuffle of a footstep in the kitchen triggered an instant reaction from Scully. In a split second, all hell broke lose as Scully let go with a round of fire. It was the fourth of July all over again when both men blasted away at each other. Then silence fell over the apartment as the two searched for each other in the dark with their keen eyes. Scully heard a quiet movement from the kitchen and pointed all his senses in that direction. Crouching low, Scully bombarded his would be killer with a steady stream of death.

A mighty thud sounded, silencing a heartbeat.

Scully lay on the floor afraid to breathe, afraid to move, until he fired one more time. His round wasn't returned and he breathed easier while he crawled into the doorway of the kitchen and fingered his way up the wall to the light switch. He sensed that it was safe to flick the switch.

A flood of light filled the room. But, in Scully's eyes, the sight of death mushroomed the closer he looked.

It didn't take long for him to recognize the body sprawled across the black and white linoleum.

"Holy shit! The big Palooka!" he whispered, not wanting the neighbors to hear any more than they already heard.

"Parrini's strong arm!"

Scully used his foot and his hand to push the lump of death over. A bloody .38 lay beneath him and blood gurgled from his chest like oil seeping from an oil well.

"Dead, Jack, stone dead!" Scully's forehead was

covered with beads of sweat. If he could only tell his heart to slow down or his hands to stop shaking, he could think better but he couldn't do either. Instead he headed for the last corner of his half gallon of wine. The red liquid trickled down his throat, easing the tension along the way.

It wouldn't be long before Parrini would send some more of his boys crashing down on him. There was no doubt in his mind that they'd be ready to do Carla in, too.

The documents were scattered on the dresser so that let Scully know that someone knew he hadn't come through. But how many knew it? Thinking time had run out and the only thing left to do was split and fast!

After scooping up a few rags he darted out the door and into the car. Heads popped from behind curtains and cracked doors but Scully didn't see anything except the bright street lights.

By the time he got to Carla's he had convinced himself that there would be no way to talk his way out. It didn't matter what color he was, he'd crossed the underworld.

Bang! Bang! Bang! crashed his fist against Joyce's door. The sound shocked Carla and Joyce and puzzled looks flashed across their faces.

When Carla opened the door, her eyes widened.

"Scully, what the . . ."

"Ain't got no time! Just throw some things in a bag and let's split!"

"But! But!" she stammered.

"No time for buts. Get your ass movin!"

"I can't just leave." Her arms were flying in the air. "You betta tell me what this shit is all about!"

Scully didn't have a second to waste. So he pushed Carla up the stairs.

Joyce stood gawking at the two of them screaming at each other. They ran down as fast as they went up.

"Now, just a damn minute!" Joyce yelled with her hands on her hips. "Somebody better say something that makes sense."

"Dig, Joyce, some cats' on my ass and Carla's too. That's all you need to know. If I tell you more, they'll be on your ass, too."

Joyce's eyes bucked.

"Well, what do you want me to do?"

The wheels in Scully's head began to turn again as he shoved his hand in her face.

"Give me your keys!"

"What!" both girls said.

"Yes, damn it, cough 'em up!"

With keys in hand they zoomed out the door. There was so much that Joyce and Carla wanted to say to each other. If it was their last goodbye it was a hell of a way to end a friendship. Instead of saying anything, they had hugged each other until Scully pulled Carla out the door.

Tears filled up in her eyes but she was too frightened to cry.

"Don't start that shit!" Scully warned as he zoomed toward the freeway.

"Everything's gonna be cool, just don't panic!"

"Panic! It's too late to do that!" she cried, holding her face in her hands.

"We may have a chance. The cops'll be looking for the Chevy, but . . ."

"But what?" she asked, not really wanting to know.

Scully clammed up and drove toward the San Diego Freeway. He kept checking out the rearview mirror. If she'd only signed they'd have been straight. There must have been more to this deal than he knew. Otherwise, they wouldn't have sent the big guy to do him in. When he asked for twenty grand to set up an office and do some promo work, they'd said no deal. He figured they wouldn't give him the dough. They had only trusted him with three grand. Not enough to shit with, he thought to himself. He had stashed that on himself but he wasn't ready to spill it to Carla.

The lights of the freeway whizzed through the car as they headed south. If a car was following them, he couldn't tell but he was checking everything.

Sixty, sixty-five, seventy read the speedometer.

"Cool it, Scully! We'll get stopped by the cops!" she warned.

"That may be our best bet!"

Seventy-five eighty, and finally a steady seventy-five when Scully checked out the gas gauge. He relaxed a little but kept both hands on the wheel.

"Light me a weed, baby," he asked with his eyes on the lines in the road.

"You're gonna need some sleep so let me give it to you now." It was rough for him to tell her all the shit but he knew he couldn't keep it from her. He blew a puff of smoke into the steering wheel and rapped on.

"I been dealin' in drugs for, shit, too long. That's why I didn't want to leave the steel mill. Red tried to get me busted, but it didn't work. They fixed him and got me out. Baby, I know too much so they got me out of town with some jive shit 'bout wanting to get into films usin' me and *you.* You were supposed to sign them damn papers but you backed out. Well, you didn't know and I couldn't tell you that they'd kill me if you didn't. I still ain't gonna look like no chump in front of my woman. No fuckin' honky's gonna use my woman no mo' and if it means it's gonna be me and them, then that's what it is!"

Carla sat with her eyes closed, blocking out the world.

"You mean that they'd wanna kill you because I didn't sign those papers?"

Scully crushed the cigarette in the ashtray as he drove into the night at a steady pace.

"Baby, hustlin' is all I know. You can take me out of Gary, but I'll hustle some damn place else and when they sent me out here with three grand, that was all I needed. I didn't make no trips to Gary. Only once. The time I called you, they were puttin' the pressure on me by that time. There's twenty-five grand on the way to Mexico that belongs to us and we're on our way to get it."

Carla almost sprang out of the car.

"What? twenty-five what?"

"There it is," he smiled. "My cut buddy, Duz, from Gary, is headin' on down the road. Man, I been settin' this stuff up since I got here. What the hell would I look like in the movies. I wasn't gonna let them use me like they wanted. My plans were to get out here, close enough to Mexico, make a quick kill and split. I'd figured you'd be too big for them to touch. That's where I went wrong. I would have left you, but I had to face facts. They would have killed you."

"Baby, hookin' up with you was my first mistake," she said sadly. "But lovin' you was my biggest mistake."

"Hey, easy on that love shit. Them kinda ties I don't need. Just be my woman. You start talkin' love and I be thinkin' you wanna get married. And marriage ain't nothin' but headaches for a dude like me."

"Humph, you've just shoved my career out the window, you know."

"Yeah, I don't even want to rap about that. I had to decide for both of us and when you dealin' with heavy dudes you don't have time to decide."

Joyce was probably calling Ben, and all hell would break loose once he found out, Carla thought.

"Scully, maybe you can just put me out in . . ."

"Put you out!" he looked at her hard. "You must be jivin'. I'm savin' your ass, woman!"

Carla was so confused and tired that she couldn't think. She tried to let the words roll out without giving much thought but even that didn't work.

"You talkin' 'bout lovin' somebody, then you talkin' 'bout gettin' out like this is a small town bus line. Baby, you don't get out when you want to, you get out when I say you get out!"

The pressure was on Scully and Carla was getting the blunt end of it. High beams from the rear brightened the inside of the Mustang. Carla's head jerked around.

"The cops?" she asked in fright.

Scully pressed down on the acellerator. The engine roared louder and louder.

"Naw, that ain't them." He stretched his neck to get a better look out the mirror. "That's one of Parrini's men!"

"What'll we do?" Carla trembled. If the nightmare would only end! If she could just shake herself and start all over.

There was nothing left to do except press on. Scully zoomed up the freeway, trying to outrace death, but the sleek black Lincoln was dead on his ass. For two miles the cars weaved and bobbed through the light traffic and Scully tried like hell to outrace the dudes.

"Baby, stop shaking and get down! Fast!!" he ordered.

Carla's head hit the torn seat cover as Scully swerved to avoid hitting a tractor trailer. She couldn't see him make fast moves, but she felt as if she were on a roller coaster with her eyes closed.

"What are they doing, Scully?" she trembled.

"They trying to run us off the road, the bastards! But they just playing with us. They could have taken us a long time ago!"

The deadly .44 magnum was ready and its mighty shells were a squeeze away from the Lincoln as it rammed Scully's car in the rear.

"Baby," Carla popped up.

"You betta hold on. We're gonna try and get off at this exit at the last minute!"

"What?"

"Don't ask shit! Just do!"

Bam! Bam! Bam! The back window of the Mustang was shattered by a 3030 Winchester. In a split second Carla's head was on the seat but Scully couldn't move as fast. His right shoulder burned with pain when a shell ripped at his bone.

"Motherfucker!" he yelled.

The car was alongside Scully but the exit looked further away while Scully fought to keep control of the car. He shot wildly out the window but no damage was done to the Lincoln. Gunfire was hot and heavy just as Scully swerved off at the exit. The Lincoln was too far to the left to make the quick turn but Scully was bleeding badly and in too much pain to keep control of the car.

Scre-e-e-ch, Crash! Boom! Down the side of the hairpin curve rolled the Mustang in a fiery ball. Over and over until it landed at the bottom to its cool, grassy death.

There wasn't time to scream. There wasn't time for last minute anythings! Scully had played with death, trying to save his life and Carla's, too! But the burning desire for power would never be his.

He believed strong enough, though. He knew he could take a chunk of this world and wind up calling the shots. Power was all that mattered to deal with the white world! He played the game the only way he could but his time ran out.

The crackling fire cut the midnight silence as the car burned out of control. There was no chance for Scully. His body had burned instantly.

Carla's badly bruised body lay fifty feet from the wreck. Two truck drivers rushed to the scene and covered her body with a blanket as a police siren grew closer.

"Jesus Christ!" one hefty trucker yelled in shock. "This chick looks like she ain't gonna make it!"

"Yeah. Besides probably being in a coma, it looks like she's broke a few bones."

"There's no hope for the driver."

The police ambulance whizzed Carla to the hospital, minutes away, its siren blasting loudly. It wasn't until she was rushed into the Emergency Ward that a black nurse peered through the mud caked on her face and recognized her.

"That's Carla Brown!" the nurse gasped as she stared at the jelly-like body. "Call the chief surgeon, quick!"

For four and a half hours they worked on the movie queen, patching, cutting, digging and scrap-

By Bobbye B. Vance

ing until she was wheeled to the recovery room.

Ben had heard the news on television and rushed out of the city to the hospital. The doctors told him she was barely alive but she'd pull through.

For three weeks Carla lay in a coma. Flowers, telegrams and messages filled every corner of her otherwise sterile private room.

Ben and Joyce stayed with her day and night. Scully didn't matter. His murderers didn't matter. Just Carla mattered.

"I'm going to get some coffee," whispered Joyce with tears in her eyes.

Ben just shook his head.

The room was silent. The sight of three-quarters of Carla's body in bandages frightened the hell out of him. He couldn't deal with it and walked slowly to the window to stare at the Christmas lights in the distance.

"She doesn't even know it's Christmas," he said tearfully. "She doesn't even know her picture was a smash."

Grief had swallowed up every inch of his body. MERRY CHRISTMAS, HAPPY NEW YEAR flashed on and off for the world to enjoy but for Carla Brown there was only the seemingly endless sleep.

"Oh," a voice peeped. "Oh."

The voice didn't register with Ben right away

but when the bell did ring in his head, his mouth flew open and a smile flashed on his face. His heart fluttered with joy as he rushed to Carla's side.

"Carla, Carla, baby," he laughed nervously. "Carla! Oh, Carla!" he yelled. "Can you hear me?" He wanted her to talk her ass off so he blasted her with questions.

Her eyes blinked slowly and her dry lips quivered. A nurse rushed in with Joyce when they heard Ben's voice. They held on to each other with happiness and relief.

"She might make it," the white nurse whispered with a broad smile. "She just might make it!"

It was just before New Year's Eve when Carla spoke clearly. The bandages were still wrapped around her and her legs were in traction but she was definitely getting it together.

"And Scully?" she asked Ben who sat faithfully by her bedside each day.

"Scully's dead," he answered sadly.

Carla only turned her head slowly to the Christmas tree that was aglow with blue lights and a sea of gifts.

"But you're here and you're gonna make it," He reassured her as he poked gently at her pillow.

"I don't know," she sighed. "I'm so tired of fighting and not getting any place. Look at me. I'm

By Bobbye B. Vance

at the top and I can't even enjoy it." She looked into Ben's eyes.

"Do you think I'll ever work again, Ben? Do you really think I'll work again?"

Ben smiled. "The Doc says six months. If you just keep on pushin'."

"Ha, ha, ha!" laughed Carla. "That's easy to say. He's not in this bed. Ben, I really don't want to live anymore," she whispered. "It's hard work. Hmph. It's even harder than acting and I don't want to do that anymore."

"Why, Carla, why?" he asked with deep concern.

Tears filled her eyes when she tried to speak. Pains stabbed at her throat and cheeks as tears started to flow.

"I used to be bubbly Clara Brown, remember? From Gary, Indiana, with a hell of a lot of plans and hopes and dreams. Then I came out here thinking everyone wanted the best for me. But I got put in a trick bag. It's done something to me. It's made me hard, cold and evil. That's not me, Ben." She paused to clear her throat. "Even Scully didn't give a damn about me. I don't think I'll ever be in another film. They'll forget me by then."

"That's a lie, Carla. Look at all this. They won't forget you!"

"You really think so?" she asked with interest.

213

"Don't ever lose sight of that star. I told you life's a bitch, but you don't give up. Don't let it get the best of you. We love you, Carla. We want you. And most important, I want you."

Carla frowned and smiled all at the same time.

"You want me, Ben? After all the shit I put you through?"

"Yeah, woman!" he laughed.

"But, I'm an invalid and nobody has time for me. I'll just . . ."

"You're only an invalid if you let yourself be one. All black folks are invalids if you wanna know somethin'. That's why we gotta pull together to help each other over the hump. Besides, you're an invalid as long as you let your mind tell your body that."

Carla was quiet for a few more minutes. Her eyes were getting heavy. Ben stroked her arm softly.

"What about making a better life for yourself? This time, lean on me? We'll do another flick."

"You sure?" she asked. Her eyes were closed now.

"I'm sure," he whispered.

"You know that script Les had from Karen what's-her-name? I'd like to do that. It was a love story. By a woman, for a change!"

They laughed.

"And, maybe there's a part for Joyce?" she asked as she held his hand.

"Whatever you say, Clara Brown. You're the star!"

San Francisco Nights

Faye was on the verge of having everything she'd always wanted . . . riches, fame, acknowledgement as a scientist. She'd come a long way from her poor Kentucky upbringing.

Even love was in the offing when rich, powerful Bradley Tate came to San Francisco. He was handsome, dangerous, and determined to have Faye . . . but only on his terms.

Very quickly, Faye found herself on the verge of losing everything: Bradley Tate, the respect of her partner, and the friendship of the baseball player, James "Bluegrass" Oldham, whom she'd always thought of as a little brother. She had to fight for survival—without knowing the rules of the game . . . a deadly game!

EUDORA CARROLL grew up in Kentucky and, until recently, lived in San Francisco. This is her first book with Heartline . . . but we're sure it won't be her last!

Love's Fire & Glory

Fanita Moore was young, beautiful and rich. Her mother, Tallahasse Moore, had fought her way up from poverty in the South to wealth and social prominence in New York. Tallahasse adored her beautiful daughter and was determined to give her the best of everything. She had Fanita's entire future planned: the golden success and proper marriage that she envisioned for her daughter would also be the crown jewel in Tallahasse's own glorious life and career.

This is a rich and exciting story that ranges from the deep South to New York to the gilded salons of Europe between the wars. It is a story of fortunes made, squandered and regained. A story of love lost and recaptured. Above all, it is a story that will penetrate the consciousness of anyone who has ever loved, been loved, or simply dreamed of love in all its glory.

Lover's Holiday

Brandy Hollis was on the verge of the kind of success she always dreamed of. Her photographs were being given a major exhibit in Los Angeles. The man behind the exhibition was handsome Raymond Beasley. Raymond had the power to move mountains for her, and Brandy secretly loved him. But Raymon seemed only interested in her as an artist, not as a woman.

Then Brandy encountered Lawrence Parker—a man who made it immediately clear that he responded to both the artist and the woman. A man who desired her with every fiber of his being. Suddenly she was caught in a web of tangled emotions that threatened to destroy completely her chance for happiness, or, if she made the right choice, assure her of a golden future of love and success

HE'S BAD . . . HE'S BLACK . . .
HE'S RADCLIFF

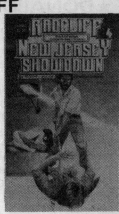

THE BLACK EXPERIENCE FROM HOLLOWAY HOUSE

★ ICEBERG SLIM

AIRTIGHT WILLIE & ME (BH031)	$2.25
NAKED SOUL OF ICEBERG SLIM (BH709)	2.75
PIMP: THE STORY OF MY LIFE (BH806)	2.95
LONG WHITE CON (BH030)	2.25
DEATH WISH (BH075)	2.25
TRICK BABY (BH807)	2.95
MAMA BLACK WIDOW (BH808)	2.95

★ DONALD GOINES

BLACK GIRL LOST (BH042)	$2.25
DADDY COOL (BH041)	2.25
ELDORADO RED (BH067)	2.25
STREET PLAYERS (BH034)	2.25
INNER CITY HOODLUM (BH033)	2.25
BLACK GANGSTER (BH028)	2.25
CRIME PARTNERS (BH029)	2.25
SWAMP MAN (BH026)	2.25
NEVER DIE ALONE (BH018)	2.25
WHITE MAN'S JUSTICE BLACK MAN'S GRIEF (BH027)	2.25
KENYATTA'S LAST HIT (BH024)	2.25
KENYATTA'S ESCAPE (BH071)	2.25
CRY REVENGE (BH069)	2.25
DEATH LIST (BH070)	2.25
WHORESON (BH046)	2.25
DOPEFIEND (BH044)	2.25
DONALD WRITES NO MORE (BH017)	2.25
(A Biography of Donald Goines by Eddie Stone)	

CURRENT HEARTLINE ROMANCES
SEE SPECIAL
FREE
BOOK OFFER
ON REVERSE OF THIS PAGE

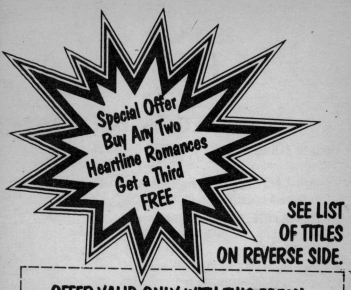

Special Offer
Buy Any Two
Heartline Romances
Get a Third
FREE

**SEE LIST
OF TITLES
ON REVERSE SIDE.**